Where I've Been

Where I've Been

short stories

Kim L. Dulaney

Third World Press
Chicago

Third World Press
Publishers since 1967
Chicago

First Edition
Printed in the United States of America

Cover and Text Layout Designer: Relana Johnson

Library of Congress Control Number: 2008904271

ISBN 10: 0-88378-302-9
ISBN 13: 978-0-88378-302-3

12 11 10 09 08 6 5 4 3 2 1

Contents

Truth is in the Details ---- 1

Simple ---- 3

The Faucet ---- 6

Cleaving to the Man ---- 7

A Summer of Sundays ---- 13

Queen for a Day ---- 20

Sweet Pea and 'em ---- 22

Lost on Do Nothing ---- 25

One Hundred and Twenty Raindrops ---- 31

Red—The Color of Passion ---- 35

Getting to Know Him ---- 39

What's in a Name? ---- 42

Watching the Break Up ---- 47

The Plunder ---- 49

A Cold, Cold World ---- 53

Where I've Been ---- 56

Chicken ---- 60

The Mark of Johnny-B-Gentle ---- 69

Whining ---- 72

Pretty Feet ---- 75

Truth is in the Details

I could give you details. I could say that after you called me the other night and told me what you told me, I wasn't really shook up, just angry. Could say I knew exactly what to do this time.

I could argue that he must have put the red-haired woman right out of his car, or even left her there in the parking lot of Ecstasy, the club where you saw him and her "frolicking."

I could tell you he came in around 2 A.M.: only about thirty minutes after the time you saw him and called me.

Could tell you that I nearly killed him with the shoe I threw when he opened the door. Could say he was so drunk and unstable that when the three inch heel clucked upside his head, it knocked him back into the wall; then he slid down against the wall to the floor. Could say he earled with wretched convulsions sitting there on that floor, against the wall, as I threw all his stuff: his tailored suits, and his Bottinos, the brown ones, the black ones, the tan ones, and the blue ones into his chest and his pond of *boys night out* lies and the dinner I could tell included spinach dip, probably Papino's—his favorite.

Could tell you that once I had piled all the things I thought I couldn't sell or give away, on his slumped over drunken body, I pushed that jerk and our fifteen year history out the door, out the house, and out of my life forever, for real.

I could tell you that. Or I could tell you it was more like 5 or 6A.M. when he got home. Could say I heard his key before it opened the door. Could say I quickly wiped the tears from my eyes and pretended to be sleep. Could say my pillowcase was soaked and made me imagine I was drowning and couldn't breathe. Could tell you that he undressed and put his Bottinos on the shoe rack, in their proper place, his suit in the dry cleaners bin, and his shirt in the light colored to-be-laundered bin.

I could tell you that he cleared his throat several times while brushing his teeth and washing his balls in the bathroom with the door partly cracked. Could tell you I watched him, looking much like he looked when we met at 23. Could tell you he washed like he washed at 25, while I shouted and cried at his back, back then. Could tell you he still lifted and scrubbed underneath like he did at 30 and 31 and at 32 when someone said the woman he was with favored and could have been my favorite cousin Celine. Could say that at 35 his washing changed, but only slightly; he didn't scrub so hard anymore, didn't always remove all traces of their womanish funk. Could say that at 37 when he gave me Chlamydia, his lax cleaning might have been the cause, but because he cried and swore he had accidentally picked up and worn someone else's contaminated jock strap at his Tues./Thurs. intramural pick-up basketball tournament, I stayed.

Could say I was still there after I saw him wash lightly twice between 37 and 38 because I was trying to finish graduate school, and had no money and no job. Could say the night you called me and let me hear his laughter through your cell phone while the picture downloaded then transmitted his tongue visibly tied between his and her lips, I first pretended to be sleep, then at some point after he really was, I put my body spoon-style into his, and placed his arm around me needing to feel his warmth.

I could tell you his body, that always saluted me years ago, was less than excited by the feel of my firmness, kept tight and taut for him. Could say he slept well and solid the entire night. Could say I have yet to exceed sleep two hours at a time since that last episode. I could really tell you I almost died there in his arms, drowning in sorrow and disappointment. Could say I floated in our leaky boat too long, and when I finally left with nothing but a single wooden oar, I found the courage to swim to shore.

But that was four nights ago and at nearly 39 my memory sometimes fails me, so I'll just say—I left.

Simple

The questions had been fairly simple. They hadn't asked her one thing she couldn't answer. P.C. Birmingham was pleasantly surprised, yet still slightly uncomfortable. This was her first time meeting her readers. After her third book hit the *New York Times* Best Sellers List her publisher had said it was necessary. She stood behind the podium at the front of the room, her small arms anchored on the angled wood top, lifting her just high enough to see the more than 300 people who filled the theater-like seats and lined the walls like a geometric-patterned wallpaper. P.C. was a mother and homemaker from Grand Junction, Michigan. The big city attention from kids young enough to be her own, unnerved her. She watched the flow of energy in the room in amazement. Never in her life had she seen such a fuss over nothing.

A woman with exaggerated and excessive movements made her way to the mic located in the center of the aisle midway up the stairs. "Well, I just wanted to tell you I love your work. You are a genius, Mrs. Birmingham!" The scattered-haired woman shouted into the mic causing a piercing screech. The room cringed. The woman bashfully tucked into herself, smiling as her hair disappeared into the colors and spots that were people.

"Thank you." P.C. replied.

Then a man whose head seemed as high as the ceiling appeared. The mic became a toothpick against the girth of his massive upperbody. "Mrs. Birmingham," the man said, his voice echoing up and out of the ceiling, "you are so layered and complex in your simplicity. Your writing is quite terse and synoptic, your characters are multidimensional, yet, uncannily familiar—how do you manage it?"

P.C. smiled, took a deep breath then offered, "Well, I first have to tell you this. I'm so nervous up here I'm peeing my pants."

The audience laughed politely.

P. C. fidgeted with her book a bit before proceeding. When she finally spoke, her voice was warm and small, much like the trickle of urine she could feel seeping its way down her inner thigh.

"Well, I'll tell you this, and then I'ma have to leave," she said as she crossed her legs tightly trying to temporarily seal the leak that had troubled her off-and-on since the day of her 62nd birthday.

"Most of my characters come from folks I don't even know. I got that Earl character from the eyes of a man in the grocery store."

A few giggles scattered the room. P.C. appreciated the smiles that filled their faces.

She scratched her scalp, just above her right ear. "And that Lucille came from the legs of the young woman, uh, that lives down the street from me, who uh, woke me up when she came strutting home at 2A.M. one morning." She raised and shook her disciplinary pointer finger in the air.

The crowd responded with movement, no giggles, no smiles, no Amens, no nothing.

"The *Price Is Right* gave me Juanita." The pitch of her voice peaked and her eyebrows raised as if the audience should've already known that.

"Harry Belafonte" she smiled, "Harry introduced me to Allen," she paused, "you all remember Allen, the abolitionist in Narksonville." She nodded her head, like a college graduate school professor, confident that his students would be familiar with at least the basics.

"And if my memory serves me correctly," her words came slowly. Her eyes reached up into the files of her mind and she bit at the right corner of her bottom lip, "a cardinal, yeah, must have been," she waited a second, "well, I can't be sure, but it was some sort of small breed bird that told me about Savonia—"

P.C. stopped abruptly. The warmth was spreading. She could feel it somewhere near her knees. Soon she would have to have her favorite new shoes cleaned. She might even be forced to throw them out—well, if they stained too badly. Pee could do that. She peeked down at her shoes, reminding herself they were indeed too fragile to survive the likes of a saturated piss.

She looked behind her to her left, then her right, trying to determine the course she'd take to save her stretchy, cloth, tan colored shoes. Just before she was ready to face her challenge, she turned quickly to the podium, lifted herself to meet the mic, and prepared to hurriedly shush the folks and thank them for buying her books.

But they were already silent.

Not a person spoke or even moved. It seemed they needed more. P.C. was thrown off. She had to go! What would she say now? Quickly! She couldn't just leave. But the heat was growing past her calf, threatening to exceed the length of her leg. Her feet began to pulse. Her ankles warmed. Her entire body was like a furnace, threatening to reduce all but her bones to ashes! All at the thought of piss in her new shoes.

Her tiny body sank behind the wood structure that supported her. As she melted into defeat she noticed the posters that framed the room. They were pictures of authors. Authors she didn't know or hadn't read. Authors whose names and book titles had apparently meant something to the folks gathered beneath their images.

Always alerted by impulse, P.C. read the first name she could manage. "Hemingway!" She yelled almost in a cry. "I studied Hemingway!"

The crowd burst into applause. The people jumped to their feet. The cheers were so loud P.C. Birmingham could hear them above the cascading rivers of her piss, on the first floor in the women's washroom, in the last stall, perched in a squat a few inches above the rim of the public toilet seat, in her still dry, new shoes.

The Faucet

The water kept dripping. Slowly. The quiet in the room blended with the plumber's nerves and guided his chocolate mounds of muscle. Drip. Drip.

The faucet stretched toward him, seemingly wanting to touch him—feel his masculinity. She had to be a witch, shiny and glistening, taking all of his attention, with her long slender neck, and her thick widened bottom.

Drip. Drip. Drip.

I wondered if he knew I hadn't been womanized in a while. Wondered if he could smell my God's fertility stagnant in my middle. Wondered if the faucet was trying to drip my secrets in his ear.

Drip. Drip. Drip. Drip.

I watched his hands caress that slut. Watched him give her grips she could never reciprocate. Heard him say her water was hot and he could feel her—as if the heat that burned my blood for him paled in comparison.

Drip. Drip.

"I need to fill this pitcher," I whispered. I tried to drain her—kill her blaze—cool her down, placing her neck towards cold and my bosom next to his face.

His mouth widened from surprise or the pressure of my hip on his shoulder as he stooped, hands still beneath the sink.

Drip. Drip. Drip. Drip. Drip. Drip. Drip...

She spilled quickly. Then the hussy struck back: she filled and exploded! I yelled as the man-stealing tramp sprayed her pinned-up flow in my face, squelching the full service call the plumber could have satisfied.

Cleaving to the Man

Lucille paused in the middle of the hallway just outside of her room. Which way would she go? To the left there were people scrubbing walls and mopping the floor. To the right someone was high upon a ladder trying to balance a long slender box and replace fluorescent bulbs at the same time. Lucille could see someone's jeans and white and neon colored sneakers protruding beyond the wall as the person kneeled in the entryway making final adjustments to the Christmas tree and decorative packages beneath it. For a moment she thought of sitting herself right in one of the matching antique wing-armed chairs positioned on either side of the cherry lettered John Hockton Retirement Home sign that graced the wall right in front of the door to the place. But it was cold and she didn't have long underpants and other proper gear for the weather. Lucille needed to think rationally.

"Hurry up!" A woman in a white uniform, white shoes, and light blue smock hurried past where Lucille stood. "The police have already begun to surround the property, which means the president should be here soon."

Another woman in the same white outfit, same white shoes, with a lime green smock with pink and black stethoscopes haphazardly pictured all over it, stuck her head around the corner and yelled, "Where is the candy for the dish at the front desk?"

"Ask Joe." The first woman yelled back as she exited the far end of the hall. "And tell the RNs to make sure everybody is dry and clean in the next twenty minutes." The woman disappeared through a door, but her voice could still be heard as the door closed. "Put Mr. Linbomb to bed—an injection if need be."

A man in waterblue scrubs with a white mask resting beneath his chin came from the room next to Lucille's and grabbed her arm. "Come on, Ms. Lucille, you heard her. We gotta get your diaper changed." He pulled.

"I haven't soiled myself, young man. Let go of me."

"It's been a couple of hours since breakfast time. You had to do something by now." The man placed both hands on Lucille's arm and again he pulled. "Let's go."

Lucille didn't budge. "I didn't eat breakfast, and I haven't soiled myself." Lucille stiffened her body. "I've been getting ready for the president. Now take your hands off of me, so I can situate myself."

The man leaned in close and took a long sniff.

Lucille's nose shrank into itself from the man's odor. The man dared to sniff her when he had a stench that could mangle a maggot. The man smelled like a mixture of smoke, urine, and butt; similar to the way Lucille's oldest son had smelled when he had allowed a badly bred hoodlum to convince him to take up smoking cigarettes when he was barely sixteen. Lucille didn't try to hide her dissatisfaction with the man's smell. "Uhhhh," she moaned.

"Well, alright," the man said, "but you need to get out of this hallway. Go to your room, the health facility, or the rec room. They don't want nobody wandering around today." Then as quickly as he appeared, the man disappeared.

Where would she go? Where would he likely go? Lucille thought. The medical wing? No. With its broken equipment, its overworked, and under qualified staff—which was all the John Hockton Retirement Home could afford, even when the president of the United States was expected as a guest—the medical wing was not a spot for the president to take pictures aiming to boost his approval rating. Not at all. He wouldn't go there. Lucille turned right, her shoulders leading her forward towards the recreation room. It was the only place void of glaring inadequacies. She followed the pale pink walls to the vomit green door. She hated the colors of the place, though they had, on her bad days when she couldn't remember room numbers, served as reminders of what was where.

Lucille pressed the door and it opened easily. Most of the other residents needed help, but Lucille, though she was seventy, could still bench press fifty pounds of steel, and she could walk more than thirty minutes on the treadmill. In fact, Lucille had walked twice a day since the day she'd heard the news that the president would be visiting the retirement home. For four long days Lucille walked once in the morning and once at night, and she'd spent an unusually long time lifting sand filled weights and squeezing the pressurized gadgets meant to help arthritis. Her efforts paid off. Beneath her elastic waist polyester pants and the oversized red sweater with green Christmas trees tracking the length of her arms, Lucille's stubby little body seemed stout and rebuilt. She felt stronger than ever.

"Lucille!" Mr. Barney yelled. "What did they tell you about walking 'round here by yourself? I have a good mind to tell mama!" Mr. Barney shook his pointed finger towards Lucille's direction. "Ain't no tellin' what's in those woods. They got that other gal. You won't stop 'till we find your narrow, unruly, disobedient tail beneath one of them old oaks." He pouted and turned his twisted face towards the wall.

Lucille ignored him. She knew that she was not Mr. Barney's sister, whose name was also Lucille, and she knew they were in Evanston, Illinois, not Mississippi or some other rural area that Mr. Barney's mind visited whenever he saw her, or heard someone call her name. Plus, Lucille had too much on her mind. She had no time for Mr. Barney. She had to prepare herself for the president. She chose a seat near the front of the room; an unavoidable spot. The president would have to pass her.

President Pine couldn't have known how determined Lucille was to meet him. He couldn't have known the lengths to which she'd gone to make his acquaintance. How was he to know that she was the grandmother of Private Marcus Walt Johnson? Afterall, Lucille's last name was Eaglefoot, her grandson didn't even bear her same last name. Though the president met many young men and women who served in the armed forces, Lucille hoped he would remember Marcus. She would have to remember to make the Sir name distinction when she spoke about her grandson to the President.

She wore the sweater Marcus bought her for Christmas last year with some of the money his parents gave him as a high school graduation gift. She wished she could find her picture of him. She would describe him. She would mention Marcus' dimpled smile, and his bright brown eyes. President Pine could not have met many men who had eyes as wide and clear as Lucille's grandson, Marcus.

Lucille's face was expressionless as she heard the crowd rustling in the hall. They were definitely moving in the direction of the rec room where she waited. She could hear the pounding rhythm of their heels increasing in volume. She could almost picture feet landing on, and just outside of the red lines that striped the floor in the halls of the west wing of the building. Then almost all at once, the rhythm stopped. Lucille sat at attention. She thought of making her way to the hall. She wondered if someone had peered into the room, noticed her uncanny resemblance to her grandson, and decided it best that they visit a different area of the facility.

Then she saw the men in black. They entered the room and quickly dispersed around its circumference. They looked up and down, around, behind, and over things as if searching for something. One man who wore a funny looking earpiece, unlike any Lucille had ever seen before, appeared to speak to himself, maybe chanting along with the song that could have been playing on the strangely shaped ear thing he wore. Lucky for the man he stopped speaking to himself just before the group encircling the president made its way into the room.

Lucille watched them all carefully. Her sight was a little fuzzy because she hadn't taken her blood pressure medicine for more than two months. Since the day Marcus had been brutally murdered in Iraq, less than a year after he had joined the United States Army, Lucille had hidden the pills that were given to her with her breakfast, and the ones she was supposed to take with her dinner. She'd dropped them in her socks and kept them there until she could slip them into her pillowcase with the other nightly bedtime doses of valium and muscle relaxers she pretended to take. And each night Lucille lay her head on those prickly pills and rested assured that her time was coming. No one but Lucille knew her plan. Not the people at the retirement home, not her children or her grandchildren, not even God; because there was no God to tell. Lucille had realized the God she'd thought she'd known her entire life was nothing more than an illusion. He disappeared when she needed him most; when her grandson needed him most. So, either God had never existed, or He'd been overthrown by the demons of President Pine.

President Pine was a short, petite man. Without his title he would have surely been powerless. Here he was being lauded and feared. He was making his way around the room, bending to shake hands that couldn't reach up, placing his hands on shoulders that drooped lifelessly as a result of cuts he'd made to medical programs, smiling and cracking jokes as if there was cause to celebrate his policies, and consoling people, spreading "holiday love" to lonely elders whose family members were busy working two jobs, or jobless and even homeless under the pressure of the happy president's depreciating economy.

"God bless you," he kept saying.

The camera flashes kept popping off, like firecrackers, or shots exploding in the eyes of the old people. Lucille squinted, but refused to close her eyes. She didn't want the man to vanish. She needed to ask him a few questions. So when he finally arrived in the space in front of her, she lowered her head, slumped her back slightly and barely lifted her hand from the arm of her chair, as if she didn't possess the strength of her harbored pain. As she had hoped, the president bent down to take her hand. When she could feel his warmth firmly planted in her palm, she held on tight. Her grip caused him to squat. The cameras kept flashing. A smile was plastered across the man's face.

"Wow. You've got some grip here." He reached his free hand over and loosened Lucille's grasp. "God bless—" He said as he prepared to move to the woman seated next to Lucille.

But his words were choked by Lucille's grip on his throat.

His men rushed to his aid. They grabbed her arms, but his yell stopped their efforts.

"Wait! Wait! Her nails are in my throat."

Lucille had not thought of that idea. She had not known her unattended-to nails would be used as a weapon. She saw the man's face turning red. Beyond his face she saw the American flag on a pole in a far corner of the room. It had not been there before his visit. She had not seen a flag since Marcus' funeral, except for in bad dreams. Marcus' funeral had been a collage of red, white, and blue. No dimples, no face. Just a casket covered in the red, white, and blue. And the fabric that engulfed the entire event, flowing in the wind, draping the colors, the red, white, and blue over Marcus' memory. The other details of the day of the funeral were fragmented. She'd heard talk of a medal and honors: heard her daughter mumble something about hanging some honor from her mantle. She remembered wondering how people could give a medal in exchange for a missing upper body. Wondered how her children and grandchildren figured they would "feel" Marcus' presence through a small piece of scrap. Lucille wanted Marcus' heart. It was missing. They said it had been blown away from his body. Her dear, sweet, Marcus.

"Where's his heart?" Lucille's crackling voice growled. "My grandson's heart. Where is it?" Her nails dug deeper into President Pine's neck.

The president must have realized Lucille had no plans of releasing his throat. He must have thought she was crazed. He surely could have yanked her hand away from his neck, but the claws were pulling his skin, and the cameras were flashing, and the broadcast was live. His widened eyes signaled for help.

"Cameras off!" The man with the headphone yelled as men pushed the media through the small space past the vomit green door.

Lucille watched them. The president's eyes, then the men as they did things, most of which never even registered in her mind. Then the nurses held her, as one of them quickly pushed the needle into her arm. Almost instantly, she was unable to speak. She was never able to tell the president that Marcus didn't like to fight. Never told him that once, in the fourth grade, Marcus won class president and announced that he had plans to be president of the United States after he finished earning a law degree. She never told him about the mark on Marcus' chest, right over his heart; the one he got when he fell from the tree trying to get her cat, Fluffy down.

The president never asked God to bless her. He never told her where Marcus' heart had gone. He just rushed from the room with his hand pressed to his neck. Lucille hoped he would bring it back to her.

As the nurses emptied her tired, rumpled body into her bed, pills spilled from her pillowcase onto the floor and their shoes. Lucille didn't care. Pain from wounds inflicted by the many men who smashed the left side of her body against the floor made her feel as if half of her had been crushed beneath a truck. The pain was almost unbearable, but Lucille didn't cry. In fact she smiled. She was thinking of the package she would receive from the president: Marcus' heart. It would probably be a big box. It should be put in the grave with him. *Everyone should have a heart,* Lucille thought. She hoped it would come before Christmas. Hoped it would be packaged in wrapping as bright as Marcus' eyes had been. She imagined a big ornate bow that would symbolize the life Marcus had lived. And though she thought she didn't believe anymore, she prayed for no red, white, or blue.

A Summer of Sundays

Week 8—

"I wouldn't have believed it eight weeks ago!" Pastor Hughes says when he hugs me. He's grinning and yelling my name, "MC Swiper! MC Swiper!," holding my hand high in the air. The sound of the crowd is deafening. The church people are wilding out: stompin', clappin', and even dancin' in the isles of the sanctuary. I won the contest. I hadn't planned to, didn't want to, but I did. Pastor picked me up from the hospital Sunday, the morning of August 25th, and took me back to the room in his house, where I'd stayed the whole summer. He signed the papers releasing me from his custody. Then after I cleaned myself up, he brought me to the church. I didn't know why. Then when he brought me up front, I saw the trophy, and the people all stood up. Now, I see my Mama rushing up the aisle, towards the pulpit. She's smiling and moving her lips real wide. I can hardly tell what she's tryin' to say. Pastor translates for me, "It's a boy! You got a son, man!" He pats me on my back. I feel big! In two month's time I am more than I've ever been: a son, a man, a father, and a winner; all while I was locked under somebody else's command. Seems to me like my God is smarter than I thought, like He's the greatest gangster I've ever known, so I bow down and step away, leaving Him alone on His throne.

Week 7—

Mercedes is blacker than usual. She's looking crazy as hell, much older than just twenty-five, but I still feel weak when I see her. I want to cuff her under my wing and fly away. She's a ride-or-die chick, but she's scared. I can see it in her face. I wonder if she can tell I can't catch her this time. She's throwin' looks and pain I can't hold. I feel the urge to grab somebody and make them absorb it; make them suck it up and fix it. But it ain't nobody's fault, and ain't nothin' nobody can do. Truthfully, I think it's God punishing me for punishing the freaky dude that messed with the little girl. Maybe I went too far. I didn't mean to kill dude. I warned him twice, then dude muscled up and came at me. I wish I could take it back. Just drop a dime from a phone on a corner somewhere, and let them dudes in the joint take care of him. Wish God would let go of my child's neck, stop making him pay for me, like I paid for my daddy, and he paid for his.

I get in the bed with Mercedes—right in front of the pastor. I want to feel what we made between us. I wrap my arms around her stomach and hold her tight, too tight. I want to give my seed my life, try to push it through the skin that's between me and Mercedes. I don't need it no more; I did all I can do with it.

The last thing I remember is Pastor Hughes putting his hands on us: me and Mercedes' head. He prayed. I prayed too. Then I woke up there, in the bed with my girl, and the pastor was gone. He stayed gone the whole week. Deacons and church ladies brought us food. We couldn't eat much, but I appreciated it.

Week 6—

Pastor Hughes ain't as soft as he looks. He caught me on 95th street, passing the projects. Him, the dude from the movie, and a couple of big, swoll' deacons grabbed me peek-a-boo style: jumped out of the Caddy and snatched me. I thought they were gonna trunk me: fold my six-foot, one hundred and eighty pounds, pack me up, and toss the key—thought pastor thought I took something of his. I was only trying to go save mine. I need to be with Mercedes, need to go give life to my child.

They take me to the church and sit me on a pew. Pastor telling me why I don't want to mess this thing up. He say it's gonna end in a couple of weeks—Hold on—I'm thinking I won't have no reason to be free in a couple of weeks. And I'm telling myself I shouldn't kill church people, especially in the church house. Then this smiley chick comes over and hands me the paper with the lyrics I wrote. She says my turn is coming up, and I have to read. I don't talk 'cause I can't. I'm dying inside 'cause my baby dying and my girl is by herself. Then the lady calls my name and she points to me, and the people all clap and wait like they waiting to hear a word from God, or something. I ain't got one. Matter of fact, I ain't got nothing left in me. I'm sitting in the center of the church, two rows from the front, all eyes on me, then I feel a hand on my shoulder. It's the pastor. He gets in my ear, telling me kids admire me and are watching. I still don't talk. I can't. Then he whispers, "I'll take you to see your girlfriend myself. Just say something to the kids."

I get up fast and think of something, 'cause I know I can't read what I wrote on the paper. I think to myself, *God is good,* and I say that, "God is good." Then I just give it like I'm getting it. "God is good. When your family, friends and the crowds are all gon,' and you packing up to leave yourself alone, be strong, 'cause God is good. When your world gets bigger than your back can hold, and the game grows cold, and thuggin' gets old, God is good. He'll bring you what you need, and get you where you need to go. Hold on. Give Him a chance." Then I thought about my shorty and I ask more than I say, "Give Him a chance." I ain't cry, but my voice might've cracked a time or two. I wasn't too concerned about it; I figured I could make a brick bleed if it would water my seed.

Week 5—

I want to die. I've done everything I could for everybody I love. I believe in God and do His work: feeding folks, clothing folks, checkin' fools. I ain't never wronged nobody that ain't wronged me first. And now *my* seed might not make it? I'm paying out the ears for doctors, vitamins and organic food—all b.s.! My Mama said doctors got Mercedes, my girl, on bed rest. They say the baby is distressed, but they can't take him from her womb now; things are too unstable. Mercedes' mother called my Mama, blaming me. She ain't even there with her own daughter; at home hugging the pipe and got the nerve to judge me. She said Mercedes is stressed and worried about me. She also called me a murderer, told my mother she don't care what the court says, or who took the blame for me, she knows I'm guilty, knows I killed that dude. Since she knows so much, she should know I'm planning how I'm gonna kill her. She told my mother I ain't never gonna be nothing but a murderer—said I'm killing my own unborn child, and don't even know it. You don't say stuff like that to somebody's Mama.

Week 4—

They asked me to compete in their speech contest. I'm supposed to write something, submit it to the pastor and then read it in front of a church full of folks next month. These people have been pretty good to me, I don't want to be rude, or offend them or nothing, but I don't talk like they talk. And even though I've come to understand that we all pretty much the same—we all got issues, and struggles, but the way I deal with mine is different. And when I'm done with this summer of Sundays, the clock in my world is gonna strike twelve. My chariot ain't gonna "swing low", it's gonna change into a pumpkin, and I'm gonna have to walk home; back through the hood where I come from.

So, I go to the pastor and try to get out of it. Pastor Hughes ain't havin' it. He tells me to write what I "feel compelled to write." He said "Don't be nervous, son, God will guide you." It's the first time a man has called me 'son', so I don't give him no drama. I just leave. I'm feeling like a punk, letting people I don't even know tell me what to do, and how to do it; my Mama ain't never even been allowed to do that. I wonder about the consequences of fighting against this writing competition thing; will the church people report me to the judge? Wonder if I'll get locked down just 'cause I don't wanna write a punk poem. My girl's about to drop a load; my shorty will be here in a few. I ain't tryin' to be locked up when my shorty comes, so I go somewhere and write what I know, like I know it.

In this life you get what you can take. God is a gangster. He don't roll with cowards and punks. If you're scared to stand up, God will stand back, and let people walk right over you. If you ain't got the heart to make the world respect you, then God wants you to get out of the way; make room for the Swiper 'cause I'm coming through—by any means necessary I'm gon' get mine.

Swipin' Monday through Sunday, rain or shine, I gotta get mine.

Like Jesus, I was born with enemies. The man was out to destroy me, before he could even know me; gunning for me; scared of me. God sent me to a manger on fifty-third street. No heat. No running water. Mama was in church crying and waiting. Daddy ran away hiding and dating; making more of me, showing me what I shouldn't be. No room in the inn? I built my own. Just like the song—God bless… well, you know the rest.

Swipin' Monday through Sunday, rain or shine, I gotta get mine, gotta get mine, I gotta get mine…

Week 3—

I finally got the balls to look in that brown bag the pastor always carries. I found out dude prefers Gin to Pepsi. Now I understand everything: why the secretary cops it for him, and why she delivers it behind closed doors, midday, when his wife ain't home, and I understand why the pastor cries like he laughs: barely and briefly.

These people ain't all bad. A couple of days ago, I rode with an old dude who quoted Tupac and KRS1. I was curious about that, thought the dude went and memorized a few verses just to try to manipulate my mind. So I asked him a few questions. Dude was on point. I wondered if the church folks knew they had a mole in the system. Then dude took me, as a chaperone, to take some kids to see that movie, *Akeelah and the Bee.* Those were some bad kids. I wanted to smack 'em and tell 'em to stop talking so much. They were missing the message in the flick about believing in one's self. But they weren't my kids, and it wasn't my money that paid for them to see the joint.

When I got back to my room, I kept wondering about the dude from the church. How old was he? Where did he come from? How did he trick off and wind up at New Baptist? I wasn't gonna ask like a lame, so I figured it out for myself. Dude must've been at least ten years older than me, maybe thirty-nine, forty. He evidently was from Chicago, 'cause he knew a lot about every southside neighborhood we passed through, even mine, on our way to the suburban theater. And he might've got with the church folks the same way I did — caught a case. He must've had a hellava sentence, 'cause dude functioning like he been in this church scene a while.

Week 2—

I'm cramped in that little basement room at the pastor's house. It reminds me of my first spot I copped when I left my Mama's spot. I thought it was huge back then: my own bed, my own washroom, my own phone. I don't have a phone here, though. It ain't allowed, according to the program rules. The pastor is real strict about sticking to the rules. He says I'm his responsibility and if he is caught allowing me to break rules, then he will catch his own case. I don't know why he volunteered to help me out. It sort of irritates me — this dude coming to my rescue like he's some kind of friggin' hero, like my live-or-die is in his hands, like he's some sort of good that's better than me. His wife cooks breakfast every morning, and calls me to come eat, like I'm their kid and we the Huxtables. I wanna tell her I don't get up before ten, but when she calls I'm usually hungry and ain't got nothing else to do, so I don't say nothing. We read, or they read aloud, a bible verse every morning before we eat. She got fresh flowers on the table, petals dropping off near the platter of freshly sliced fruit. I'm just gonna try to stick this thing out; stay focused on what I'm trying to do, which is to get back to my life.

Last night we went to something they call a "revival." It was like a big party. I ain't never seen, or heard of church people doing the electric slide in church. Not only that, this place had honeys. Chicks looking like they come straight out of an Outkast video. I was charged up. I don't know if the thighs on the honey next to me, the singing chick with the Mary J. Blige body, or the fact that I hadn't seen my girl, had me going, but I definitely was excited about something. And they do this every year? I gotta put the date in my Blackberry and make a point to stop through next year, when my life is back straight.

Week 1—

Standing in front of the judge, and next to this Pastor Hughes, I'm wondering if I made the right choice. The judge refers to me as an R&B star. The pastor calls me a rapper. *I'm a lyricist dummies*, I think to myself. Then the judge says I'm released into the custody of, blah, blah, blah…effective Sunday, July 1st, and that I have to live with this dude for sixty days. It's supposed to be a community service assignment, but it sounds more like house arrest. The judge is a Black man who is friends with the pastor; he says he hopes I learn something while I'm teaching something at the church. I can't imagine what they want me to teach a bunch of boring little goofies. I don't know scriptures, don't believe in the White man's bible or his God, and can't stomach ignorant Black folks who claim to live by it.

The judge pounds his little hammer on his desk, like he gets the last word. I'm thinking, *yeh, for now, only for now.* On our way out the sheriff near the door speaks to the pastor and the pastor gives the dude a soul handshake. He's probably telling him to set me up, or make it hard for me, 'cause if I fail out of the program my time doubles. But these dudes don't know who they messin' with; I've done street time under homies, and in situations these dudes can't imagine–you'll never see this on TV.

When we finally leave the courthouse, photographers are waiting. They're snapping pictures and asking stupid questions. 'Did I do it?' Like I'm gonna just haul off and holla out, Hell yeh! I did the job none of you punk-ass cowards were willing to do, and I'll do it again!"

Queen for a Day

I see it, she thought to herself, leaning close to the mirror. Peering deep into her own eyes she thought she got a glimpse of what he must have been staring at. He was all the time smiling, looking at *it*. *It* was that thing that made him want to sit and hold her, read to her, sing to her. *It* was the something that made tears fill his eyes and his kiss, like sugar water. She had never seen *it* before, never thought there was more than the dark circles that surrounded her eyes, her full lips, and the sides of her wide nose. Never understood why he seemed to enjoy caressing the hairs her mama had called "nappy," even the kitchen with its "steel wool." She fingered the tightly wound clumps gathered at the nape of her neck—they felt beautiful in his space, his presence just beyond the restroom door.

"You okay?" he called to her.

His voice sounded as caring as men in movies who were paid handsomely to love their long, straight-haired, thin co-stars.

"I'll be right out," she almost sang, his orchestra playing in her mind, Spanish guitar highlighted. All of life with him was melodic. She straightened her striped ten dollar top. He loved the orange and beige colors against her caramel colored skin. The mirror was the bass beneath his words that kept crooning in her mind. "You are beautiful," is what he'd said. How he said it without blinking, or smiling, or looking away, is what she remembered most. And now she saw much of *it*. She saw the way her eyebrows underlined her thoughts, just as he had described. Saw how her lips were simply large replicas of her eyes. Saw the veins in her neck; they looked like thin columns supporting a fancy strong jaw-lined statue, just like he said. *Beautiful*. She stretched in admiration.

"Hello!" Someone knocked at the door. The drumline blended with the days' melody and almost went unnoticed. "My daughter has to go." A voice shouted. "Please hurry!"

She turned on the water, spraying it against the sink, splashes against the tiny tiles on the wall behind it. Her cloth purse caught splotches that were sure to stain. *Memories of the him that can't last,* she thought while rubbing suds between her palms, beneath the warmth of the water and his expectancy.

"Adella" he beckoned. "You okay, Adella?" Close to the door, above the ranting of the female stranger and her kid, he called, "Adellllllla."

She leaned against the door feeling the vibration of his wanting her. Slowly, her paper towel lined grip turned the knob. She glanced a last time in the mirror and breathed in all that was her as he had detailed, trying to preserve *it*: the thing that had birthed her at thirty-two, full grown and woman.

"Sorry" she said, opening the door.

The toddler and woman pushed quickly past her.

He stood waiting between the table where their food sat already arranged in front of the place each was to be seated, and the bathroom where she seemed to have almost lost herself.

"Thought you might have snuck out of a window or something, on me." The sight of his teeth like piano keys tickled something deep in her soul.

"Never that." The silent music dropped low. Everything slowed. *Who was directing this thing,* she wondered. *Which ancestor?* Everything was perfect. Her feet barely touching the ground, she made her way into the booth.

He situated himself across from her. It was electric: their sounds, the lights, the mood, the isolated window seat in the back corner—most everything. Save for the young cashier's loud, brash periodic repetitive inquiry, "Welcome to White Castle. May I take your order?" the date would have been perfect.

Sweet Pea and 'em

Sweet Pea and 'em gathered on the sidewalk in front of the yellow frame house. Punkin was there. Baby Girl was there. Pooh and Lil Bit were there too. All were shouting at the top of themselves. *Had Sweet Pea gotten out at four hundred, fifty-two or sixty-two? Had the clothesline jump rope clapped against itself at the top, above her head as she did her mumbles, or had it nicked the bottom of her slightly worn green Allstars?*

Baby Girl swore on her mama. She saw Lil Bit's right hand bump into her left. "Ain't even no need to argue about it," she said, drawing her cheeks in, forcing her lips to pucker. "Y'all know Lil Bit is double-handed. Sweet Pea should get another turn, and she should start from four hundred sixty-two!" With that Baby Girl left the circle. She pushed her way past Punkin, careful not to touch Lil Bit.

"I ain't double-handed." Lil Bit's squeaky voice rose above the others. "Sweet Pea just got big feet. Her foot landed right on the rope!" Lil Bit's right hand squeezed her waist, cranking her head higher and higher with her tightening grip. "Y'all just want her to win! She can't even jump! Just 'cause she got on those shoes? In my Jeepers I jump better than that."

Pooh grabbed Lil' Bit's free arm, pulling the arm and pointed finger away from Sweet Pea's face. "My sister ain't double-handed. Me and my Mama taught her how to turn double-dutch." Pooh bucked her eyes. "Y'all trying to say I can't turn, or even my Mama can't turn double-dutch?! I know y'all ain't trying to say my Mama can't turn double-dutch."

The girls were momentarily silent.

Baby Girl turned towards Punkin. She had to bend her body to look around Pooh, because the top of her head was about level with Pooh's shoulder, and she couldn't see over the big girl. "Punkin what did you see? Didn't you see the rope collapse at the top?"

The circle broke. Everyone faced Punkin. She was silent. Her head tilted towards the ground where she could see the bottoms of

Sweet Pea's green and yellow plaid elephant bell pants, resting just near the top of the blue star on the side of the flat rubber-soled green shoes. It was the same star she had watched hop and pop up from two to four hundred and fifty-two. How Punkin had wished she had them—the shoes. The pants. All of the pretty things Sweet Pea possessed. How she wished she owned the clothesline so all the girls would want to be her friend, and come in front of her house which was all the way at the other end of the block. Then she could become better at jumping rope. She could jump all night, and wouldn't have to stop and go home when the street lights came on.

"You heard her! Stop standing there like a bump on a log—like you are crazy or something. Didn't you see the girl step on the rope?" Pooh moved in close to Punkin. "I know you saw her foot on the rope." Her breath warmed Punkin's forehead.

Sweet Pea gathered the rope, holding it in the middle; looping it at either end.

Punkin's eyes moved to Pooh's torn PF Flyers. "I wasn't watching," she murmured.

"Oh, you was watching. You always watching everything. You saw her foot hit the rope." Pooh's flat chest pushed against the side of Punkin's face.

Punkin leaned away from Pooh's body, triggering Pooh's step in closer, then Punkin's step away, and Pooh's step up closer again, until the two spinned in slow motion, small face to big flat chest.

Sweet Pea who had moved to less than a foot away from her bottom front step of the house, gripped the rope tightly.

"Leave her alone, Pooh. You can't make her say she saw something she didn't see." Baby Girl moved closer to the twirling girls. "Come on, Punkin." She pulled at the back of Punkin's shirt. "You don't have to say you seen what you didn't see."

"What did you see, little girl? Huh? Is Sweet Pea out, or what?" Pooh spit when she talked. Her first few splashes landed on Punkin's face and went unnoticed. Then, in unison with her final words, her spit splashed down on Punkin's cheek.

"Ugh!" Punkin shouted and she leaned into Pooh's chest, rubbing her face against the girl's faded shirt.

Pooh immediately drew her arms back and up, revealing the

hole beneath her armpit. She would have pummeled Punkin, as she had most other girls in the neighborhood, save for Punkin's tight grip around her body. She swung into the girl's back as best she could with the girl's head tucked tightly into her underarm.

Sweet Pea, noticing Punkin's small body nowhere on the ground, stopped running, and eased back down her steps. Clinging to the rope, she moved over next to the tussling girls. Baby Girl had already stepped in front of Lil Bit, impeding her interference. "Fair fight!" She yelled as soon as the two girls became entangled. Lil bit dared not tussle with Baby Girl. Baby Girl was taller and thicker than Lil Bit, and she had three sisters and four brothers, all older, and all bigger and stronger than she was.

With everyone accounted for Sweet Pea squeezed her eyes closed and charged at Pooh. She flung her hands high in the air, spinning each one in quick circles like blades on a fan. Pooh and Punkin's bodies fit just between the spinning blades. The rope Sweet Pea was holding opened out and over the top of the girls, landing around Pooh's neck. Pooh's swinging fists stopped. She grabbed at the rope that tightened with each winding spin of Sweet Pea's arms. Punkin broke free and ran. Now Sweet Pea, noticing the void on Punkin's side of the mound of girl that was Pooh, yelled as loud as she could, and swung her bladed arms as fast as she could.

With her eyes still closed, Sweet Pea was lifted away from Pooh's body. When she could see again, she was seated on her bottom porch step. In the grass a few feet away she saw Pooh, Lil Bit and an unidentifiable big boy snatching and pulling at the rope that tangled Pooh's neck and what seemed like her entire body.

"Leave the rope in the yard!" Sweat Pea yelled back as she leaped up the stairs, two-by-two. She yanked the yellow paneled storm door, entered her house, and latched both the top and bottom locks. She watched them untangle the rope for what must have been three minutes. When they had gathered their bikes and left, rope lying in the yard, Sweet Pea watched. She stood behind the latched door watching her new rope for hours, contemplating a dash to retrieve it, hoping Pooh and Lil Bit had gone to play on their own block, praying Pooh wouldn't seek revenge, and wondering if she should've just admitted she'd stepped on the rope, when the count was only almost four hundred sixty-two.

Lost on Do Nothing

Me and Lucky standing at the corner of Fifteenth and Hard Times Blvd. We minding our own business. Dude pull up in a brown Lexus or Cadillac: one of them 'I-done-freaked-over-somebody-and-lucked-up-on-some-loot' rides, and he asks us if we know where Do Nothing Street meets Effort Avenue. We tell him we ain't never heard of no Do Nothing Street. He say, "What do you mean, man?," then he bend down over the passenger seat on our side of the car like he think we gon' jump in the raggedy ride, and he look and point up towards the sky or the corner where the streets cross. I'm looking at this dude like he out his mind or something; I figure he must be high on some stuff. Lucky ain't paying the dude no mind. He just trying to figure out why the bottom of the Crown Royal bag ain't padded, double lined or somethin'. I look at Lucky looking at the gold thread on the bottom of the bag. I'm thinking them cheap muufuugas dun' cut back on the thread, that's all. They usin' cheaper thread on them bags. But before I can say anything to Lucky about the thread, I feel the dude in the fancy ride burning me up. He staring at me like I stare at muufuugas to get them off me, you know? Like no blinkin', tryin to catch a muufuuga eye and let-him-know-what-you-made-of type of staring. Me and Lucky used this look twenty-four-seven when we was driving trucks cross country before the company fired us and hired independents. Problem I had with dude in the shiny ride was I wasn't pushin up on him. Why the hell he starin' at me?

Me and Lucky standing at the corner of Fifteenth and Hard Times Blvd. Minding our own business and this dude rolled up on us. Now he think the world supposed to stop twirling because he lost and don't know where the hell he going. "Look, man! I just need to get to Effort Avenue. Is it east or west of here?" the fool shouts. It ain't even cold outside, a normal November noon day, no less than forty or fifty degrees. Yet, this dragon-breathed dude puffin' when he speaks, like he the king of muufuugas and his words supposed to mean so much each one needs its own cloud to carry it from his mouth to the front of My Kinda Liquor Spot where me and Lucky had been busy working till mister white shirt and striped tie rolled up. Lucky smiles and turns the bottle up. He don't even glance at this clown; that's just how important he thinks dude is. But I'm getting pissed. I step to the car. Man, what you want? Why you sitting here hollering and bringing attention to a muufuuga? Me and my man, Lucky been right here, in this same spot for months: Fifteenth and Hard Times Blvd. We ain't seen no Effort Avenue, and we ain't seen no Do Nothing Street either. I talk calmly to the dude, and instead of him listening and moving on, he starts yelling again. This time he wavin' his hands a lot, and keep pointing at the street lights. "You are on Do Nothing Avenue. Can't you read! Hard Times Blvd is on the other side of town! I grew up on Hard Times so I know exactly where that street's located." His head is all cocked to the side. "I just came from Productive Place which is a long, long way from here. I'm just trying to pick someone up." He throws his hands in the air. "The last message I have from the person who needed a ride, said he was on Do Nothing making his way towards Effort Avenue." Now he's pounding his open hand against the empty car seat. "Just tell me the direction towards Effort Avenue, guy, and I'll be out of your hair. Trust me I won't come this way again—ever."

Look, man, Me and Lucky standing here at the corner of Fifteenth and Hard Times Blvd. You the world traveler, dun come from Productive, know where Hard Times is, seem like you'd be the one to know where all the rest of them streets you need is at. We ain't bothering you and to be straight up, we wish you would stop bothering us. We busy trying to do things, man. Crown Royal bags got stitching that won't even hold five dollars in change no more. People dropping nickels instead of dimes and quarters in the shoe over there. It's real out here, man, and you driving around in yo' fancy car screwin' with people. Why don't you just go back where you came from and get directions to where you need to go? "I would if I could," he replies. "It seems while attempting to help someone, I've gotten myself lost." The dude seems frustrated. Sounds like a personal problem to me, so I don't say anything. Dude looks around the street, squinting with the sun buggin' him like he buggin' me. There's a thin female in a big thick black fur coat standing in the doorway of Pretty My Ugly Styling Salon.

The dude in the car notices her and speeds off down the street. He makes a u-turn and stops his car at the curb in front of the woman. I see a smile come over the dude's face. It quickly passes, and within minutes the dude's hand is moving wildly with his finger pointing towards the sky over the corner of Fifteenth and Hard Times. I try to get Lucky to look at the way the chick keeps flinging her hair, and rubbing her coat. Looks like she's taking bites out of the hair that keeps getting in her mouth, and it looks like she rubbing the coat to keep it closed cause everybody knows she always naked under the coat.

Lucky was busy minding our business, like I should'a been, but I'm watching this dude, wondering why he wanna come down on Fifteenth and Hard Times and get started. He disturbing the peace, stirrin' up what had already long settled. He yelling out the window like he dun lost his mind. "You people are crazy!" He swerves the front of his car around Baby Girl and her shopping cart. She in the middle of the street where she always is. The slit on the side of her plastic coat stretches out and tears up some with the wind that dude's car put on her. I'm waiting and watching 'cause if this dude would'a hit that cart with that baby under them clothes and rag covers, I'da had to give this muufuuga the whippin' he beggin' fo. Baby Girl standing in the middle of the street staring at the tail lights on his car, probably trying to figure out if dude was a UFO, the PoPo, or what. Dude's car eased back into place in front of the spot where me and Lucky still dealing with the issue of the Crown Royal bag. The car shuts off. Dude sits there. First I'm watching him, then I stop looking at the muufuuga. I think I know what he doin'. He tryin' to watch how me and Lucky do our thang. We been out here for years makin' our own way—not needing nothin' more than Lucky's disability check, our government food cards and a shoe. Dude tryin' to peep game. That lost act is just part of his gimmick. Ain't nobody lost on Hard Time Blvd. You know exactly where the hell you at over here: ain't no other place like HTB. Everybody from everywhere know that.

After about a hundred or so people go in and out of My Kinda Liquor Spot, and we dun passed about twenty nickel hits in the shoe, dude opens his car door, stands outside and puts on his long black coat. Something about the way he looks says to me he been here before. His coat brand new, but it look like it could be used as a blanket if need be.

He heads towards us. This dude dropping his swagger on the left stride like he used to ride with them El Nookies on the low end back in the day. He lookin' all around like he casin' the joint: trying to figure out what he might have to do and how. Now I'm starin' at this muufuuga—straight in the eye. Lucky lookin' up at him too. We ain't blinkin' and concentration got to be shrinkin' the front of our skulls. No b.s. No punks here. I don't know what he dun did to them dudes where he from, but I'd die for mine, and in his thirty-five years on this earth, I dun seen Lucky almost kill for his, three or four times. Curbside dude putting on black leather gloves. I'm slippin' my feet down to the front of my shoes; it's the only way to get a grip with no strings and room enough to hide a bottle of Crown behind each heel. Dude takin' long strides; this means this mark is confident, he wasn't no soldier, he had some kinda street rank—chief, or lieutenant, maybe. He plannin' to bring it straight to us. Lucky got the Crown in his hand in plain view—no bag. It's more than half full and he been holdin' it all tight, passin' it like we was on bones. Now he gripping the neck. I wanna look at him and tell him to put the bottle up: don't use it. We won't need it for this dude. It's six days before the next check and it's past Thanksgiving, folks ain't gon' want to give up no decent money for the food card. Screw this dude! We need to stretch this Crown at least till the sun goes down. But I can't say nothing to Lucky while this dude is already two hops from the big shoe we got out of the yard in front of the NBA star's house the night we saw him being carried up his steps last week. The shoe is big, and it's about half full. I need Lucky to empty the shoe into the bag, but I can't say nothin'. I can't break my stare. This dude is lookin' back and forth from me to Lucky—eye to eye, his eyebrows hangin' like awnings shielding his view. Where this dude from? I feel I can read him. Then again I can't. I stand to my feet so fast he can't even see me get up. All he know is to shift his beady eyes. I can see the shoe in the scene that's fixed in my glare. If he goes for it I'll kick his teeth clear through his head, make him bite his own back. I feel Lucky up with me. He moves to the left one or two arm lengths. Can't no man swing that wide. C'mone, muufuuga. C'mone. My hands are in my pocket. I'm grippin' a stapler I've been carrying since the bug-eyed dude with the gun took my knife a while ago. I could strike up, attach his chin to the top of his head. He got a long thin neck and a pointy face. I could break it; shatter it to pieces. I could go upside his head; right above the ear, and knock his freakin' lights out. Whatever, I had better strike first. Lucky's hand is winding that Crown bottle. We ain't waistin' that Crown. One hop from the bag, two hops from my face, he stops: on a dime like he got anti-lock brakes in his long legs. "What's up, brothers?," he say. Like we all had the same mother who screamed him out first. He looking down at us, eyes still tucked under his brows. "I don't know if you've seen the signs." He says real slow, John Wayne like. Dude is acting creepy and confused; like a serial killer with chopped off hands and knees hid in the lining of his long black coat. His finger's pointing towards the sign, but his eyes ain't moved off of mine. "Do Nothing. Plain as day." He mouths. "I need Effort, or some other street out of here." He's speakin' slow and low now: almost in a whisper. His finger is stuck up, pullin' towards the sign, raisin' higher each time this dude opens his mouth. Me and Lucky ain't sayin' anything. I ain't never seen this dude's kinda crazy before. I break my stare and quickly look up to see what's controlling this alien-type muufuuga, and I see the 'D' on the sign, then register the 'ing' as my eyes lock back into his. Lucky must've seen me cause his head is tilted. He staring at it. It's all too weird. Lucky look at me, then I look at him, and at the dude real quick like. Lucky catch the cue and watch the dude while I look more carefully at the signs. Sure enough we at the corner of Do Nothing and Just Talking. What the hell is goin' on?! I'm ready to die—caught in the matrix. Me and Lucky talked about aliens once or twice, but it was too strange, we left that alone. Now. What's this?! They ain't taking me. My head gets so clear I see what wasn't there seconds ago. Dude got something in his hand, probably a gun. At the same time I start remembering somebody talkin' about Effort Avenue (The skirt at food card place). She kept talkin' about Effort and Temporary and a bunch of other places I ain't recognize. I remember she said "to get to Effort, walk towards the hill, then go up the hill." She said the food card was supposed to give us strength to get there. I shouldn't have sold the cards. I need the strength to get my head from beneath this big dude's arm. I'm wondering where's my guy, Lucky? The dude is grumblin', "Where's Effort Avenue?!" The dude is stronger than I thought. "I'll get out of here, or all of you bastards will die!" he says. "I swear on my life!" His arm presses my face tighter. "Where's

Effort?!" he demands. I don't answer. I can't breath. I can't hear too well. I don't hear Lucky. I don't feel no fight, but my breaths. I'm getting dizzy. It's dark. I see dark brown skin in the small space of light beneath my head, around my neck, beneath this stranger's arm. My head feels light and I see specks of white. Then I give.

When I come to, I'm on a walkway. Dudes walking past me, not even pausing. Light snow is on everything all around me. It's covering the concrete path and the grass. I look up and around and way over by the street I see the back of a brown jacket. It's Lucky. He's at the corner of the block. He turns around, sees me getting up, and walks towards me. He's shaking his head. "He knocked you straight out! I thought you were dead." Lucky's still shaking his head. "He took us in his car. I don't know how I remembered, but I told him how to get here." Lucky can't keep still. He takin' steps, squatting, standing, lookin' at me, and up and down the street. "Effort is right there, man: round the corner. He put us out here, on Fifteenth and Hard Times." I reached my hand out for the Crown. Lucky was talking too fast. I needed something to help me understand. "It's gon, man." Lucky hunched his shoulders. "When he had you in the headlock I killed the rest of it." I just stared at him. Lucky was trifling as hell. He was always greedy and selfish. He can tell I'm pissed so he say, "I needed something to give me power to get you loose from that muufuuga. You see how big that big muufuuga was?" Lucky reaches his hand near eternity and I see, for the first time, how small he is. What about the shoe and the money, man? "He left it. Wouldn't let me get it. He wouldn't let me get nothin', not even my Crown bag. He just kept saying 'shut-up, you don't know what you need.' I'm telling you the dude was strange. He was huge, man. He was crazy." Then while me and Lucky standing near the corner of Fifteenth and for real Hard Times minding *own* business, a crowd of people, all men, squeeze around us and move us towards some doors that have opened under the big faded sign. We're pushed right pass the doors into the building. This time I search for signs and read all the muufuugas, every single one: "Men of Hope Mission," "No Weapons," "Out by 9A.M.," "First Come First Served." Lucky is pressed into the right side of my body and he's talking non-stop, telling me what happened with the big dude in the fancy car. I can hardly hear him. I can barely feel the crowd closed in on me. I'm too busy wondering who, and what the hell is on Effort Avenue.

One Hundred and Twenty Raindrops

The rain was too heavy. I could barely see in front of my face. Trees were bending, yoga posing in the wind. Though summer was officially over, the rain was cool, not cold. We should have known it was coming. First it started spitting. That was before we even left our meeting point at Thirty First Street. While the troop leaders gave instructions to the parent volunteers and our children, Nature had started spraying her words, telling us to move on, and take it home. We paid no attention. This Girl Scout outing had been planned months, hell, maybe years in advanced. My schedule barely permitted me time to do this type of parent/child interaction stuff, so I was mentally and physically outfitted to put in my time and bond with my nine-year-old daughter. The thought of postponing the ride never entered our minds. Plus, the rain wouldn't pose a real problem, at least not for Marcy and me. We liked the rain. We'd walked in the rain, played games, and even danced in the rain before. But not at the lakefront, not so close to where rain puffed up in arrogance, and drew power in the comfort of so many comrades. And not naked against big, not-so-friendly bully drops that played too rough and too long.

I wanted to call time out or something. The sleeve I had used to occasionally wipe the water from my eyes was soaked, and from the rain was settling in my eye sockets, stinging my contact lenses. Yet I was determined not to quit. I could rough house with the best of them. As a kid I'd pin my brother in headlocks, and my male cousins in sizzler positions that made them honor my tidbits of testosterone with yelps of "uncle" and "I give." If I could just make it around the bend that seemed no more than a mile ahead of us, then I could duck under the overpass, catch my breath, wring out the legs of my pants and the sleeve of my jogging suit, and lead the more than one hundred and twenty plus troops of young feminist time-snatchers into their first real victory. However, the rain was merciless. It beat upon our faces, punched through our socks and shoes, and soaked into our coverings leaving nothing, not even our underwear unaffected by its weight and its power.

"Keep riding!" Greg, a male volunteer with unhandicapped eyes came to our assistance. I didn't mind him leading. Though women had mapped out the route, and organized the health stops which were strategically positioned along the trail, Greg could lead us to our destination if he so desired because some situations are gender neutral, and a good set of eyes is a good set of eyes. "Just keep the bike straight!" Greg yelled. His voice navigating me past short shrubs and solid iron back benches that would have surely taken me out.

"Marcy!" I called out.

Greg's assistance and security restored my confidence and renewed my energy. I yelled out to the girls to pass on some of what I now possessed in abundance. "You all alright? Everybody O.K.?!"

"This is fun!" Someone replied. "Woo-hoo!," yelled another as she blew past me on her velvet banana seated streak of purple passion. "I could do this forever!" the small girl whose helmet leveled with my kneecap sang. Then giggles. Familiar giggles that belonged to my own Marcy seemed to hitch a ride on my back slowing me in my stride. "You okay, Ma? Isn't this great!" she yelled, her voice ricocheting off of the back of the Shedd Aquarium, over the smooth of the slick treetop leaves. "We should go further. Ma, can we go all the way to Navy Pier?"

I couldn't help but feel she was taunting me. Couldn't she see the waterfall rolling over my eyelids, cascading down the slope of my nose? Hadn't she noticed my lips blowing chimney-like puffs trying to develop a flow of sustainable breaths?

"Race you!" the mini me snarled. Her feet quickened their circular rhythm like an old school locomotive. I could hear her determination mocking a win, "I think I can, I think I can."

The possibility wasn't totally infallible, but it would have to happen some other time, in some other situation. Not only one week after she'd learned to balance a bike. It had been years since I'd straddled the steel of my old faithful Blue Thunder, and yes, the handle bars were a little off centered, and my waist fell wider than my hips were accustomed to supporting, but, hell no! Oh, hell no!

A smile cracked across my lips. I could taste rain and victory equally. I swallowed it in gulps. Yeah, she was growing up. Yes, she could almost fit my blouses, even without signs of a budding bosom. Sure, her last pair of school shoes were a woman's size six. And it was true that the day before the ride she got her first teen deodorant stick with the pink and green springtime flowers pasted like frightful reminders of growth and change all around. And so what, we shared shower caps and hair stylist, CDs, comedy and light romance fiction and flicks—so what?!

She was moving too fast!

She giggled her way between the yellow guard posts, slightly wobbling through the shallow pool at their base, conquering the frame-high mud as if it was nothing at all, as if she had been born with spoked toes. Her friends joined her giggle song. They all rushed past me, all but the one big girl who lagged behind; fussing about her lunch. The thought that her butterfly shaped peanut butter sandwich might be dampened by the downpour made her sad.

"I'll stay with you, Marcy's mom. I'm not trying to win." The girl pedaled clumsily, crucifying the dance that came natural to all bona fide bikers. "I never win at nothing," she added.

I left her. I shouldn't have, but I did.

The center-striped concrete trail moved like a treadmill beneath my wheels. I passed the girls four, sometimes five at a time. The rain no longer fazed me. I squinted with a bull's eye focus on my target—Marcy. "I'm on you, Sweetie!" I spurted before I could catch my words.

Marcy burst into laughter. With one hand covering her mouth she began to lose speed. I forged ahead. The damage was done. All that was left was to win the race.

A thunderous roar rang overhead. Then lightning stretched across the sky marking a finish line, or so I supposed. Then a "Boom!" louder than the first. Girlie screeches trailed behind me. I realized the race was over. We needed shelter. I slowed my pedaling and turned my bike towards the children. The thunder sounded again and again, the lightening seeming to chase it. I dismounted Blue Thunder and gently lay him on his side. "Leave your bikes and get next to the building." I helped corral the one hundred plus girls as quickly as I could. "Grab your lunches. Hurry!" I shouted slinging streams of water with each exaggerated motion. "Up the hill!"

Girls and leaders quickly moved towards the big black building. We nuzzled in close to the wall. There was a lip at the rooftop that shielded us like teeth in a partially opened mouth. Lakeside during the storm, we sat quietly eating our lunches, watching congratulatory waves rise to give high five to the cocky, champion rain storm.

"We could have made it, Mom," Marcy said as Taffy Apple juice squished between peanuts and caramel, her wet cheek, and her half-grown-in side tooth.

Red—The Color of Passion

This whole story is about Big Red. After Red there is no story; the tales end, the book closes.

I met Red at a club on the south side of Chicago about twenty-five years ago. When I met him he had women swinging from his neck—solid gold women strapped to big, thick, gold chains. He wore bright colored clothes with classic Dobb brims. Red was a roller.

I imagine he was drawn to me because my hair matched his skin. My stylist had streaked me reddish-orange. My curls flipped and flounced just beneath the nape of my neck, and along my shoulders and chest bone. Additionally, I wore an outfit that blended with my urban Farrah flip. My black pencil-tapered pants squeezed blood from my butt and thighs; blood that appeared as red piping down the outer seams of the seamstress straightened pants. Nothing could be tighter. Everything was as skin against my full flesh.

"You not dancing tonight?"

"I'm done. I'm ready to go home."

"What, your girl ain't had enough?"

I looked at Meeka on the dance floor. Her head was connected via her ear, to her shoulder, and her arms were both lifted like she was taping a deodorant commercial, checking for funk. Sweat ran out from under her hair and splashed against the floor in rhythm with her stomping feet.

"I don't know, but she's about to get left."

"Aw, naw," he smiled, "you would leave your girl? That's cold. You wouldn't do that, would you?"

"O.K. You'll see."

"You look too sweet to be that mean." He kept smiling. There were deep dugouts that surfaced in his cheeks when he smiled. And his teeth saluted at attention straighter than any I'd ever seen.

"Alright." I mustered an angry lift of my brows.

He leaned over the chest-high wall that surrounded the dance floor. The multi-colored flashing lights jumped from beneath the floor and splashed against his large chest. Red was so tall he made me, at five feet, seven inches, 130 pounds feel petite. His huge laugh made my voice softer, sweeter. There was no battle for dominance with Red. From the very moment we met, his presence made me want to surrender.

"You come here often?"

"Every Wednesday, just about."

"That's funny. I've never seen you here before."

I shrugged. "Maybe you been busy lookin' at something else, cause I been here."

I could feel his eyes sliding down my body.

"Naw. I guess we just been here at different times 'cause ain't no way I could've missed you." He stretched further over the ledge forcing me to face him.

I scrunched my face. "What's wrong with you?"

"You ain't watching them. They ain't doin' nothin'. Neither one of them can dance. Look at 'em."

He moved his face and Meeka was in full view. She did some scoop-type jerking move, while her partner peacocked circles around her hunched body.

I laughed so hard tears ran from my eyes. Red's too.

"They doin' better than—" I couldn't finish the sentence for laughing so much.

"Let's go outside and talk. Come on, baby." He grabbed my hand. "Your girl'll be alright. She can't leave without passing us."

The bass in the music pushed us out the door, into the first row of the parking lot, where Red's shiny Lincoln Continental occupied the first space.

We giggled beneath the stars until the last car left the lot. Then for more than twenty years we did that again and again: Red talking smack, making me laugh; me playing hard, but always giving in to Red's requests.

Until last year, Red worked overtime, plus saved a year's beer and basketball betting money to take me and the younger three of our four kids on a dream vacation. We were in Jamaica. Red was naked on the balcony. His butt rested on the railing as he showed me things trying to coerce me to join him. He'd planned the whole scene and set the place up while I showered. Candles were lit and placed around the hotel room, and on the balcony. The room smelled of strawberries. A tray with a plate of six or seven oysters sat in the center of the bed. And the clear, crisp voice of Case was crooning low through the small, but strong IPOD speakers.

In the morning, I think of you, late at night, baby, I think of you, everyday, I think of you, and eeeeeevry other day, oooooo... .

By the time I moisturized, Phyllis Hyman's *"Betcha By Golly Wow,"* the song we were married to—was playing. The horns on that track were unbelievable. For a moment I thought it was 1987. I fully expected to hear Red say, as he sometimes did back then, "You can order dessert, too tonight if you like, Big Red got you." Followed by his infectious laugh that always made me forgive the fact that he could spend a week's part-time UPS check on one night of fun, then be depressed and moody for the next couple of weeks, as his bills came due.

Red loved fun at any cost.

"Ain't nobody out here, girl. Come on."

"Man, what will we tell our kids when security walks us pass their room in handcuffs? Naked!"

"Mama and Daddy were busy loving each other when these loveless busybodies came and interrupted us. That's what you can tell them. I won't tell them nothing, cause it ain't their business. Now, would you come on here woman, my pill's gonna wear off. You're gonna miss out." He danced with himself. "Once in a lifetime thing here..."

Had it not been for the light on the building, angled above and off to the side of the place, I'd've joined him. But my forty-five fought to stay about forty, and that balcony light needed someone between twenty-three and thirty.

After a while Red came in to me. I could tell he believed he'd lost some of himself because he was unsuccessful at persuading me to join him. So he dug into his bag and pulled out a pill. He swallowed it, then swallowed a second. Then he chugged Martell and coke, our drink, like he thought his body had muscle enough to hold it. And he loved me; all night Red loved me; as deep and as best he could, he loved me for yesterday and tomorrow.

The next day Treecie, our youngest cried on the double-seat parasail ride with Red. Then Red and Niecy fell off the jet ski in the middle of the royal blue water because Red and his energy-pill-pumped mind, wanted to prove he could balance on the back of the thing while our ten year old daughter drew swirls in the waves. Then he had to meet RJ's challenge, when his namesake proved he could bungee jump more times without getting sick. Red should have stopped at five, one bungee jump for each decade of his life. But he didn't. He jumped until a knee jerked out from behind its cap, and a hip slipped, trying to escape Red's foolishness. He jumped until life left his legs limp.

So now, thrill-seeking Big Red rolls differently. He pushes the levers on his rounded base, late model wheelchair, or I push him in our Ford Windstar with the automatic lift. And we don't giggle, and I don't laugh or play hard as much. And Byron, our eldest, and Treecie, Neicy, and RJ occasionally cry openly. And I tossed Red's stamina and energy pills he gave to Byron, and the ones he was saving for RJ, in the toilet. And on evenings when his pain pills spare him a clear mind, he teaches Treecie and Niecy to pick mates according to their ability to give foot rubs and laughter. And the ground-up food that spills with Red's smack talking only makes his words slightly less smooth than when I first met him. And the stars still surround us… only now they just about gaze up at us, listening for these tales that grow up with our passing years, our children, Red's shrinking health, and my fading favorite color.

Getting to Know Him

There was a roach on the wall. It appeared out of nowhere.

My date had just arrived. He sat on the couch that leaned against the wall on which the roach crawled.

It moved upward towards the light painted-over spot where a hole had been less than four days earlier.

My date smiled. He was cute. I think he thought I was nervous. I think he figured I wondered how, or if we would get along.

I wondered what he would say if he saw the roach. I wondered if the roach would crawl onto his hands, which he stretched high above his head, if they accidentally touched the wall.

Maybe he had lived there, in the hole I filled and sealed when I knew my date would be visiting. Maybe he had gotten lost and had just finally figured his way back. Maybe he had heard rumors that his village, nestled neatly and presumably unnoticed in the wall, was under attack. Maybe he smelled the toxicity of the new super strength roach spray the exterminator had assured me would rid my small apartment of all living pests, and steered clear. Now that the candles and the dollar store cone air fresheners totally eliminated the faint spray odor, maybe he thought the eminent danger had passed.

"This is a cozy spot you have here." My date stretched his arms again; this time across the width of the back of the couch. It made him sit higher; his head probably at the feet of the roach. Suddenly I wished I hadn't put those fresh flowers in that vase, the candy in the small painted bowls, or the lasagna in the oven. "It smells heavenly," he said.

The roach moved over, as if contemplating his navigation efforts, as if the shadow my date's arms cast on the wall made the roach question his own bearings.

"Let me see your hand," I said. "I want to read your future."

"I haven't heard that in over twenty tears, since first or second grade." He smiled reaching his thick palms over the coffee table. I prayed he wouldn't bump it. The left leg was weak, and with little effort it was prone to give.

In the absence of my date's arm the roach inched downward and stopped.

I held Bobby's hand until that stilled roach moved.

Bobby would have a bright future. He'd have two, then three, and finally as many as six kids. He would marry. He would live in a clean 1800-square-foot condo. Then move to a clean 2200-square-foot house. Then a 2400-square-foot place in the suburbs. But after his fourth kid he'd move back into the city into a brick 2600 square foot home with a big yard.

It took the roach 1800 imaginary square feet, at increments of no more than 200 at a time, to move from my date's space, back to the spot on the wall he'd claimed as his own.

By 3600 square feet, Bobby had moved all across Chicago and its neighboring suburbs. He'd out grown at least seven homes with the addition of a wife and as many kids as the roach commanded. I followed him through births, first days of school, high school graduations, and marriages of three of his daughters.

Bobby didn't seem to mind. My nail and finger tip gliding softly against his palm was tolerable. So much so, he hadn't noticed the smoke.

About the time I had a premonition my date's future would include fire alarms and trucks, the roach moved. Afraid to leave Bobby alone with my uninvited guest, I waited until the smoke was clearly noticeable. "Wow! Oh my!" I sprang from my chair. "Bobby can you give me a hand?" I grabbed his hand and rushed into the kitchen. The room was filled with smoke that thickened when I opened the oven door.

"Maybe we should just leave it closed!" Bobby shouted from behind me.

Hell, no! I thought holding my breath, fanning the smoke out into the kitchen, pulling much of it with me towards the roach in the living room. "Can you get it out for me? I've got to use the washroom." *You're dead now,* I thought as I approached the front room. "The mitts are in the drawer near the wall," I yelled back as I passed the photos in the narrow hallway: my mother's, brothers', and great aunt's.

My supposed "trip to the washroom" afforded me a quick

excursion into the living room. The wall was empty. The roach was gone. I hurriedly checked the top of the back of the couch. There was no way he could have gone far. Yet, he wasn't there. He was no where to be found. As I pushed the couch back near the wall, I heard Bobby's voice in the hall. "It's okay, baby. I've been waiting for the chance to treat you to some LaGuardo's, anyway."

I met him in the hall, taking the mitts from his hands. "Thank you so much." I passed by him. "I was so into your future, I forgot I was cooking." I pulled him behind me. Once in the kitchen, I closed the oven door. "We should get out of here; give the smoke a chance to clear."

Bobby agreed.

Then as my date and I exited through the door, I saw him. He was making his way back towards the center of the wall. His brown shell moved quicker than it had all evening. I wanted to rush back, remove my flat soled sandal and smash him into the fresh coat of paint. There was no way I could do so without garnering the attention of my date, without ruining my image of loveliness. I think he knew. He circled and looped all about the off white wall, seemingly dancing and partying on my pride. His pace quickened as I flicked off the light and closed the door. I think maybe he knew it was safe, knew I would do anything to make a good impression.

What's in a Name?

The boy climbed into the third chair positioned along the wall beneath the row of windows. His eyes caught glimpse of the toy that lay in the corner of the sill a short distance from the hand he placed on the wall to balance himself. He did not touch the toy, but recorded information regarding its look and location so he could ask permission to play with it as soon as he and his mother were settled in their seats.

His mother sat in the seat beside him. The boy turned to her prepared to ask for the blue and red caped action figure that waited by the window, but his mother seemed tired and/or mad. He couldn't tell. He would wait until she was calm. He sat still, hands folded in his lap.

After a minute or so of silence, his mother spoke. "When they call Edward Smith, you get up and go." She didn't look at the boy; just sort of spoke out of the side of her mouth. She was acting strange. The boy wondered if his mother was talking to herself, as she had on the bus earlier. Then she slumped her body forward and cranked her neck around until her face was directly in front of his. "You hear me? When they call your name, Edward Smith, you get up and go and I'll come behind you."

"When they call my name?" The boy asked, unclear of his mother's instructions.

"Yes. When they call Edward Smith."

"My name is Abdul." The boy looked deep into his mother's eyes.

"Listen to me. Edward Smith."

"I'm not Edward Smitt. My name is Abdul Shabazz." The small boy's conviction echoed through the crowded pale peach painted room.

The woman froze in motion. People stared.

The woman reached over and pinched a piece of lint from the right side of the heavy crease that split the center of the nursery school aged boy's beige pants. Then she straightened the shoulders on the brown, white, and thin blue striped loops that ringed around the boys neatly tucked in cotton shirt. "What did I say? Don't show out in here. You hear me? This is serious."

The boy sat still.

The woman sat up straight in her seat. "As soon as they call your name," the woman said, aware that no one was looking, but everyone was watching, "Edward Smith," she strained, "you're gonna go."

The boy's manlike demeanor shrank. He was instantly a five-year-old kid. Carefully, he pleaded, "Go where? Ma, I'm Abdul." He reached and grabbed her wrist. "I don't want to go with Edward."

Her eyes shut. Her lips pursed together and bent to meet and fit themselves in the boy's small ear. "Abdul. Just pretend. Just for today. You are Edward Smith today." Her forehead pressed against the side of his small face.

"I don't want to be Edw—"

She quickly, but gently covered his mouth. Her lips still in his ear. "I know, Sweetie. Be a big boy. Do it for Mommy."

"I want to go with you," he reluctantly muffled into her palm.

"I'll be with you, Abdul." She paused. Eyes still closed. Forehead still warming his small face and mind. "Edward Smith. And I'm Susan Smith, your mother." She pressed her lips against his small cheek. "Okay?"

The big door beside the receptionist desk flung open. A woman marched to the edge of the door, leaned her body against its weight, thumbed through green and white labeled manilla folders and yelled, "Robert Johnson, Benjamin Brown, Edward Smith."

A couple of people moved from around the room and made their way towards the door. The mother grabbed her purse and her son's arm while her eyes were closed tightly. "C'mon," she said as she jumped to her feet. Trying not to face her son as she opened her eyes and began to pull him in the direction of the woman holding the door. The boy resisted, holding on to the arm of the chair. "LET IT GO!" The woman spoke through gritted teeth. The boy released the chair and began to cry.

"Edward Smith?" The nurse asked as the woman and boy passed through the door.

The mother nodded.

"Awwww. The little fellow is crying. You don't have to be scared of me. I'm not gonna give you a shot or anything; I'm the good nurse." She walked ahead leading the group to the rear section of the medical facility. "Johnson." She pointed to a chair. "I'm just going to get you some glasses so you can see better." She slowed in front of another seat in another cubicle with a woman seated behind a desk. "Brown." The second man sat. The nurse continued walking and talking to the little boy. "I promise I won't hurt you, what's your name? Edward right?" She looked at the boy. He sobbed openly. "Awww. We'll see if we can find you some candy when we're done. How about that?"

"Have a seat mother." The nurse walked around the desk, sat, and began typing. "You have your medical card with you?"

The mother's hands shook as she unfolded the white rectangular shaped paper and handed her borrowed, coworker's medical card to the nurse.

The nurse entered numbers from the paper into the computer. "Seven!" She looked at the mother and moved her lips, "He's small."

The mother smiled.

"Well, you're gonna have to stop crying. I need you to read some letters for me." The woman stood. "Follow me." She handed the mother the folded paper and walked into a nearby room. The mother and son followed. The nurse sat the boy on a stoop, closed the door to the room, and turned off the light. "I know you know your alphabet—you're seven years old. I can't wait to hear you read these letters." She stepped to the side. "Read that first line for me."

The boy read the letters on the chart posted on the far wall; his crackling voice growing stronger and louder with each.

"Good job." The nurse said after he'd read the first line.

The boy wiped his eyes.

"Can you read the second line for me?"

"E, G, C, N, P, T..." The five year old boy read all the letters perfectly.

"Alright, Edward! You're a smart young man." The nurse adjusted the lens on the machine in front of the boys face. "Can you read the next line?"

When the mother heard the woman call her son "Edward," she

braced herself. Then she heard her son uninterruptedly almost singing through his recital of the letters.

"R, S, N, O, V…"

After a while the nurse slid the machine from before the boys face. "High five, Edward." She held her hand in the air. "Great job!"

The boy slapped his hand against the nurse's.

"I'm going to have to remember you. You read so well I think you may be my doctor someday." The nurse grabbed her file and flicked on the light. She read the green label. "Edward Smith! Let me see if I can find you a piece of candy for reading so well. You gonna wait for me up front?"

"Yep!" The smiling boy jumped down from the stoop and hopped around a bit near his mother.

"Ms. Smith you can go to the front desk. His sight isn't too bad. You may be able to get his glasses today." The nurse waited for the woman.

The woman watched her son.

"Ms. Smith," the nurse called.

The woman watched her son.

"Ms. Smith!"

The startled mother jerked her head around. She stood and preceded to the front waiting room, son in tow.

The glasses were tiny, black rimmed squares. They fit the boy's face well. He wore them like a fine Harvard law degree; prancing through the lobby, seeing a bigger, better world than he was capable of seeing without them. While his mother finished receiving instructions and signing paperwork the boy experimented with steps and depth approximations. He reached for the counter. Slowly. He lifted his legs and repeatedly placed his feet on the ground as if tiptoeing through clouds. He even stretched his hand out and touched a man's pant leg.

The old man smiled. His silver-white closelycropped beard creased. "Hello young, man."

The boy snatched his hand back.

"You're looking mighty dapper with those dreadlocks."

The boy shook his head, flip-flopping the dreadlocks in model fashion. His mother pushed his shoulder slightly, reminding him of his manners.

"Thank you," the boy said.

"What's your name, son?" The man asked the question as the boy galloped towards the exit door, his mother stuffing folded papers into her cloth bag, quickly following behind him.

As they exited through the door the mother's son shouted, "Edward Smith!" causing a flow of tears that moved across and down the woman's face, pushed by the American big city wind.

Watching the Break Up

He moaned in a menacing manner.

He loved me; he said more than anything—ever.

I had never heard his cry, above, below, or beyond mine... not when my head swelled full of night dreams wet by his indifference, not when he pounded my core to the soles of my feet and forced me to walk on myself. Not ever.

His voice was unusually gentle and melodic. "Come home, honey. I need you."

I had never given in to the sound of his asking for more of me; had never been afforded the opportunity. So then when his hand lifted to his face and his pointer finger cleaned a not-yet-fallen tear from the inner corner of his eye, I simply watched. Like a poorly written movie I couldn't figure out, I watched wondering how it would end.

My heart, void of strings, played no melody for his newly acquired emotion.

And when his nostrils collapsed into themselves, sucking back the flow of built up drainage, and his pores flooded the space with lost things I'd searched for during our twelve year marriage, I watched. I didn't reach for a tissue, napkin, or towel to help clean the mess he'd made of us.

He was sweating, and out of control.

And when he looked into my eyes and saw only a reflection of himself, and when he stood and walked away from the table, groaning and swearing, clearing out the bottom of himself, ripping the lining of my love that had coated his inner person, I did nothing, but watch.

I understood I was powerless—he taught me that—I was just an artist; too simple to comprehend complex issues. So when he marched the polished wooden bottoms of his new Ferragamo shoes pass the other patrons, onto the terrace, alongside the waist high concrete railing that encompassed the sparsely formatted wrought iron table sets... and when he leaned atop the six inch wide ledge groping his stomach, crying dry tears, peeking at me from the corner of his soul-singeing beady eyes, and when he tilted the scale of his six-foot-two frame towards an unreachable heavenly prayer, I only thought of the Bible pages I'd worn ragged, and I watched. I watched the tip of his heels disappear beneath the outer edge of the fourteenth floor balcony protective wall, and kept watching until the watching lunchtime patrons shuddered and turned away grasping and clawing for believable reality and pieces of life, signifying his body had hit the ground; it was safe for me to leave the restaurant.

I placed two twenties on the table, removed my sunglasses, and pulled my fashioned bang back behind my ear. I saw the timidity of the sun as it crouched behind the clouds, afraid to rise, afraid to shine on me, afraid it could never tan the exposed bruise that layered deep through, past skin and skull, to the acetylcholine of my brain.

The Plunder

At 8A.M., on the third Sunday of the month of July, Mr. Barington awoke to find a lump beside him in his California King bed, beneath his 800-count stark white cotton sheets. At first glance the lump was unidentifiable. It was rounded like a miniature mountain, peaking at its center, amalgamating with the mattress at its base, and spreading wide at its east and west sides. Mr. Barington had not placed the lump there and was therefore alarmed by its presence. He carefully, but quickly moved away from the lump, and out of the bed.

From a safe distance, more than one hundred feet away from the bed, across the open-spaced 5,000 square ft. penthouse condo, Mr. Barington observed the lump. On occasion when the sun's rays shone brightest, it seemed the lump shook, or jiggled in response. Mr. Barington first hypothesized that the lump must have been some form of plant growth which reacted immensely to a sort of extreme accelerated photosynthesis process resulting from intense exposure granted by intimate approximation to the neighboring sun. He postulated that the growth was a member of the nonvascular plant grouping, since it appeared to have grown full and round without water or soil.

About noon day, when the nosy sun faced Barington's unit, and peered boldly through the ceiling-to-floor windows, the lump began to move. Barington could better see its form as it proceeded to partly split itself down its center and dance about from corner to corner beneath the sheets on the large bed. Barington stood and drew closer, watching every tremble and shake of the mysterious mass. When he was within distance, he stretched his hand towards the edge of the sheet which hung from the lower end of the mattress. Slowly, he moved his hand closer and closer to the sheet. Just when it seemed he would touch the sheet, Barington heard the sound of the elevator door opening behind him in his unit. He quickly drew his hand back to his side.

"Barington Barington what on earth are you doing?" The voice was that of Emille Tarp, Barington's longtime girlfriend. "It is well past noon, you are standing there stark naked, you look a wreck, and I could have sworn you were crouched over saluting the sun with your buttocks a moment ago."

Barington stood still. His eyes were transfixed on the motionless lump. He searched his mind for a logical explanation as to the predicament in which he awoke and found himself. There was none, so he said nothing. Miss Tarp busied herself removing yesterday's flowers from the crystal vase that sat in the center of the glass covered ornate African door which she had commissioned renowned artist Mteke to fashion into a formal dining room table as a fifth anniversary gift for Barington more than ten years earlier. She carried the vase across the floor to the kitchen area, rinsed it with warm water, and turned to replace it on the table. Only before she could make it back to the table, Barington's stillness and what she thought she saw as motion on his bed, caught her attention.

The water filled vase smashed against the floor sending droplets of water and sparkles of shredded glass about the room. "Barington! What is going on here? I will not tolerate another one. I have told you..." Miss Tarp began to sob. "Miss Detroit, Miss Atlanta, the video girl, that dreaded young girl from Blockbuster, and now this?!" She stood on the side of the bed with her arm extended above the rolling round mound. "Who is she, Barington?"

"It's no one. I don't know." Barington moved closer to Miss Tarp, careful to keep his distance from the lump. "I woke up this morning and she—it—was here." His hunched shoulders lifted his extended arms and open palms towards the ceiling. His eyes wide, his face completely distorted. "I swear to you, Darling, I don't know—"

"I don't want to hear it, Barington. I have a good mind to throw you and this tramp right out of this window." Miss Tarp paced the floor between the bed and the wall of window. "What does she have that I don't? Why must you keep subjecting me to such pain?"

Barington slowly eased himself into the space where she stood. He grabbed her in a gentle embrace. "Emille, I love you," he declared.

"What have I done to deserve such treatment, Barington?" She whined into the nape of his neck, her hands on his shoulders, her forearms pressed between their bodies.

Barington whispered as he stroked her hair, all the while keeping his eyes on the lump. "I promised you I would not again carry on affairs with another woman, and I swear to you I have not."

"Have not?!" Miss Tarp pulled away from Mr. Barington and rushed to the head of the bed, grabbing the sheet tightly in her small fist. Then in one quick stroke she snatched at the top sheet, pulling it up into the air as a magician does to reveal the prestige, or final phase of his trickery.

Barington watched in amazement.

"Then what do you call this?!" She quivered glaring at Barington to capture his immediate reaction. It was not as she expected.

Barington's eyes first popped in amazement, then relieved that he was correct and no woman lay, fearing exposure, beneath his covers, he sighed. "Look, dear." His arms dropped to his sides, his spine curved, and his head tilted back slightly. "That is no more than a booty. It's a booty, darling."

Miss Tarp watched the booty wiggle and jiggle. It was huge. In fact it was so big, Miss Tarp was almost sure she saw something attached to it. However, she dared not question Barington. If it were more than a booty, Barington would have immediately recognized it as such. For he was a skilled and prominent brain surgeon; his eyes were much sharper and precise than hers. Yet, she had not seen one such booty in her lifetime. Maybe once, thirty years ago when she was three or four years old and she and Barington's families visited Chicago's Cabrini Green housing complex. She could not completely rely on such a distant memory. "Well—" She faced Barington. Her mouth was wide. Her lips moved, but nothing came out.

Barington smiled. "That's what I was trying to tell you." His chest began to fill with air, and his voice dropped two or three octaves. "Booty, just a simple booty."

"Who does it belong to, Barington?" Miss Tarp spoke in a whisper.

"I honestly don't know. I don't remember receiving a gift of any sort. I can't imagine where it came from. I haven't had guests since you last visited."

"Well, it surely isn't mine! I know you are not trying to imply that I may have left it here."

"Oh no. No darling. It definitely is not yours." Barington's face scrunched. "No, no, no…" His head shook emphatically.

Miss Tarp watched Barington's lowered head move side to side.

"Well," she hesitated, "we have to get it out of here, Barington. You know I can't tolerate pests. I'll call the exterminator and get someone to come right over."

"Yes, dear." Barington moved to the bed taking the fullness of the jiggling booty in his hands. "In the meantime, I'll get rid of this thing. In fact, I'll carry it down to the trash and make sure of its proper disposal." He held the booty as best he could beneath one arm as he pulled on his pants. "We don't want this thing to infest someone else's home, and God forbid," he paused to catch his breath, "it should multiply." He rushed into the elevator. "I'll be back when the task at hand has been sufficiently dealt with. His fingertips squeezed the slipping booty, and his arms hugged it tightly to his chest, as the elevator doors hushed his rambling voice, "I will not have this thing in your presence, dear."

Miss Tarp dialed a number to reach the main office. She needed both an exterminator and a maid immediately. Barington's gorgeous home seemed ravished, she thought. It was no wonder why he had all types of nuisances and nudniks drawing near.

A Cold, Cold World

She wished she could take off her too small boots, but she was sure her feet stank. She shouldn't have put them so close to the heat. The warm air had made them sweat.

"Miss, we'll be closing in ten minutes." The clerk walked quickly and spoke loudly.

The woman sat up. The cubed foam seat slowly expanded behind her. She surveyed the floor between the restroom door, and the area where she sat. Beneath the cubicles, to the left of the wide space, she saw a large pair of fur covered Big Foot snow boots. To the right she saw a pair of bright red rubber duckies moving towards, then down the stairs.

She gathered the many books that circled the base of her seat. She had arranged them, as she always did, like a force field protecting her from the other patrons, and the life that threatened to find her. Now, she stacked them more neatly than necessary, placing their spines in perfect alignment. She moved slowly and without thought, giving total attention to the Big Boots and their lack of motion. *Did the booted person not hear the announcement? Would she, or he not respect the rules of the establishment, and the request of the clerk:* "Please gather your final selections and proceed to the checkout desk."

Out of the corner of her eyes, the woman glanced at the clock that hung high above the stacks at the far end of the room. It was 6:24.

On Mondays, Wednesdays and Friday's when the tall thin woman with the black rimmed glasses worked, she closed. Almost automatically at 6:20 she sent the clerk to make the rounds announcing the impeding closure. Then at 6:25 the lights in the Periodicals and Reference sections systematically, like falling dominos, darkened. Usually, the patrons followed the lighting, but on this, Friday the thirteen of January, things seemed unusual. The glasses-wearing woman left the building long before the clerk made the final rounds. The big Big Foot boots filled with the lady the woman eyed angrily, disobeyed the clerk's commands. She seemed to refuse to budge. It was already 6:26.

Surely the clerk would return. She may have forgotten the woman was still there, may have forgotten to check the upstairs restroom, may have just flung open the door and took a quick look, but with the big boot woman making a problem of herself, the clerk would surely call upon, and adhere to the rules: cutting off, locking and checking, and clearing out all that remained.

Praying, *Father God get rid of this lady, please!,* the woman filled her arms with books and headed towards the stacks. She would begin replacing the books, and if the clerk came, she would make herself so busy, so intent on replacing the books in their proper place, that maybe the clerk might allow her ten or twenty extra minutes away from the freezing weather.

6:27. The woman dropped a big book directly behind the lady. Nothing but pages moved. The woman, having nowhere to go, desperately needing a warm place to stay, crept up behind the lady. What would she do?

She pushed the lady's shoulder. The lady didn't move. Maybe she could pull her to the top of the steps, push her forward and send her down. 6:27 and thirty seconds. "Lady," the woman whispered. "Lady the library is closed," the woman whispered loudly in the lady's ear.

"Wha—", the startled lady awakened from her sleep with a yell the woman quickly muffled. It was 6:28. The woman thought she heard the keys, and the latches on the downstairs door. She held the lady's mouth tightly, as if her life depended on the lady's silence. The lady struggled, but couldn't break the woman's grasp.

The clerk was leaving, but was not yet gone. The lights were out in the two-story foyer. The woman again heard the keys jingling. Then they were still. Had the clerk heard the lady's yelp? *Please. Please, just leave.* The woman clasped the lady's mouth, twisted the lady's head and drowned it deep into her belly. She turned her butt to block the books that would have fallen from the cubicle. There could be no noise. She saw the snow and ice frosted on the windows. It was too cold! She couldn't go out there—not tonight. Death hovered. With all her might she smothered the lady's face. The lady's body quivered. The woman could hear the clerk's heels clicking across the concrete floor. She was at the door. The woman held tight; she glanced towards the clock. Everything stilled.

Click! 6:30. All but the woman were gone.

Where I've Been

He asked me and I said to the Opera. It was the only place I knew he wouldn't have been. He was an overworked accountant; ten minutes of idleness and he'd snore like a bear. He asked what it was about. I said, "Don Juan." It was the only one I could think of—the only one I'd seen. I "saw" the Opera, just varied scenes from the same one, so frequently, he thought I loved Opera.

I loved him. He was so sweet, and good to me. He got me season passes. I was to see every Opera that existed. He got video tapes of ones he'd read about—for me. He played sound tracks. I hated it. Didn't like Opera, only Don Juan. I couldn't tell him that. Couldn't tell him where I really went. So, I gifted the passes to my best friend, and I kept going.

To him I didn't come often enough. He liked his space, but I took aloofness to a different level, he'd said. "Girl," he called me, "everybody asked about you at Brown Bear's the other night. Rollo even brought you that movie you asked for—*Capote*." We collected movies; bootleg movies that would never be allowed in my *house*. Yet, they almost filled a wall in our small condo.

"Sweetie," I called them, because sometimes the warmth of one melted into the heat of the other, as if they were one in the same, "Did you get it for me?"

"No, I didn't get it for you," he joked. I figured those folks down at the night school would get it for you, since it seems you're more married to them than me."

I kissed his face. "It'll be over soon, Sweetie. I'm doing it for us. I promise it'll be worth it."

Night school lasted longer than he could have imagined. In fact, it often lasted through the day, and over long weekends. It was online. He couldn't have known.

"The Opera? Tonight?" Benjamin seemed irritated. "We need to get those papers together, Babe. We're running well behind, accruing penalty and interest we can't afford—well with your Opera adoration and all." I said nothing, just slipped on my stockings, then my slim black dress. "And have you decided where we'll spend our anniversary?" he asked. "Last minute airfare will kill us." He was so completely accurate, always planning and pre-planning.

"I'm thinking of taking on a second job," I tell him.

"I rarely see you now," he whines.

"I know Sweetie, but with our investments and all the things we're trying to do, I just feel I should help out more. It'll only be for a short while."

So much time with Mark: talking, ordering in, and hanging out. He wants to become more involved in my education; he feels like he hasn't been as supportive as he could; he promises to attend my next out-of-town conference.

I make my mornings near midnights; leaving Ben at daybreak for "early runs." Mark works graveyard shift at the auto manufacturing factory. He arrives at our building with me as I finish *the run* I need, but have no time to take. Long days steal my fervor. Ben is at the office early and leaves late, working to secure our future. Evenings are easy: three or four hours short.

Full of me, with nothing for me, my life moves along. I've gained eight pounds, eating for two, him and him. Running from our suburban four bedroom mini-mansion to our two bedroom, south loop third floor condo. My love is hazy, secure, pleasant and bountiful.

Three years and it is spring. I should have graduated by now; could have traveled to every corner of America and found every operatic production there ever was—twice. But the flowers are blooming, and the rain keeps mating with the sun, and we are with child.

Running has taken its toll. The doctor recommends bed rest—now I'm losing. My weight dropped in the first trimester—twelve pounds. Seems I can't hold the things I so badly need. Both ultrasounds, given at both hospitals, ordered by both doctors, say it's a boy. Already he's "Sweetie."

Pale green and yellow walls in the upstairs bedroom at the far end of the hall. A large vivid clown portrait on one wall, a wedding portrait of us—Ben and I, above the changing table, a bright yellow, blue, and green abacus on the tiny white dresser, and the records for the college fund account on the left side, in the top drawer. Ben thinks he'd like a Benjamin.

An old style bassinet adorned with the frilliest powder blue lace I could find; right next to our bed. A race car set, a miniature Ford Explorer, and a collection of Marvin Gaye's Greatest Hits to play on the baseball shaped CD player that sits on the sill, in the room that will be his, once we move some things into storage. He is due in September, around Mark's deceased dad's birthday. His father visited him in his dreams. He congratulated Mark; he called our baby "Albert," it was his grandfather's name—he was Jamaican.

The sun is mid-July hot. Ben turns the air conditioning high and he reads to him all the time. Mark prefers fans, open windows, and ballads. Sweetie likes it. He seems to know his daddies' voices. My belly is as round and full as the largest melon the market back home has ever seen.

Rubbing my feet, Ben says to me "You are so predictable and good. Are you ever angered, nervous, unsure?"

I answer solemnly, "Every blue moon."

On Friday, August 1st, I get a call from my mother. She has spoken to my father. They feel I should have the baby at home. I go from house to condo the full length of a week, wondering if I should oblige. Life is good, but can it last? If the baby is not home, as my family tradition warrants, I will shame, and dishonor the love my parents now question.

I watch cable television for the first time—it's the weather station. The sun is bright and there are no clouds seemingly anywhere around the world, but the weatherman predicts the showing of a blue moon. It will show down on us in about a week.

Ben's father has invited us to dinner. It is the first time. Since I am carrying them, my wrapped head, and brown skin is now acceptable. My thick tongue speaks a language of unity. White and Black; we are family.

Yesterday we received the beautiful ornate umbilical cord box. It is bright and colorful and small but sturdy. Mark has begun a search for apple trees. His family preferred Mango, but there were none. His mother has reminded him of the tradition. She will come for Sweetie's birth, and she will ask the doctor for the placenta; it is up to Mark to find the tree under which to bury it.

My family prefers plantains.

I have memories. And the money I was able to save before my marriages. Nothing else belongs to me; not even our child.

It is the last week in August. In two weeks I will see Sweetie in ways I have only imagined.

At different times each of them ask me, and I say "To work." When I go to the travel agency, to the bank to transfer funds, to the store to get tennis shoes and old Tupac cds for my younger brothers, and lipstick and hair accessories to take to my cousins, it is all work.

Today Ben's family dinner party will begin at eight. Mark's mom's plane will land around the same time. So it is that I am *working* in Chicago's O'Hare Airport, hoping for no delays, waiting to board the plane that will fly to the familiar land of Africa—Cameroon, where Baba Israel, my aging father, awaits my arrival, deserving the only male child that can carry forward Egbe, his father's, father's, infinite fathers' name.

Chicken

Jarnell was never home when the murders occurred. It took me a while to realize that was why I was so afraid. The neighborhood was changing; there had been five deaths, three in the last two months alone. Nights like this were routine now: Jarnell and me lying in bed; him face down; his arm extended across my waist; my body still, and motionless beneath the news and his love.

Channel 5 described the woman as an African American mother of three. Channel 7 called her a thirty-two year old nurse, and single mother of three. The woman's mother was on Channel 9. She could barely speak through her crying. She said her only daughter was a "good Christian woman, who loved everybody, had no enemies, and was raising three beautiful daughters, ages two, five, and seven, all by herself—and she was doing a wonderful job at it." She cried out "Why?" and repeatedly asked "Who would do a thing like this?!"

That was Friday when they found the woman's body. Saturday the policeman spoke. The woman had been sexually assaulted and strangled with some type of thin rope. They believed she had been murdered somewhere nearby, then dropped in the forest preserve in the nearby Chicago suburb where she was found.

Jarnell moved slightly, tightening his hold on my body. He was still asleep, plus he hated the news, so I turned the volume low. I flicked through all of the channels, but there was nothing else to be said about the woman. The Bulls lost. There was a drug bust on Seventy-fifth Street over east somewhere. County budget cuts were forcing four of the five southside medical clinics to shut down. And the sixteen year old Caucasian girl from Skokie had been found. She had purchased a ticket and took a trip to England to meet a boy she met on the internet. They found her by tracking her passport.

His leg crooked over my body right beneath my waist. He was so protective of me, even in his sleep. He wanted me close, as if I would float away if he didn't know where I was at all times. To ease his mind,

I never went anywhere. I didn't have many friends and was out of contact with most of my family. It was just Jarnell and me as he often said "against the world." But it was a shrinking world, and I was beginning to think it would one day swallow me whole, as it had those other women—all five of them.

At first I thought it was all coincidence. Jarnell's ice pick was missing from the garage. No one had been to the house. Who could have taken it? Then the one they flashed on the news; the red painted wood handle with the chipped base, found near the body the day Jarnell and I drove to the Dells for an afternoon of snowmobiling. The woman, age forty-two, ten years older than me, had been left naked behind a dumpster in an alley near a building in the Roseland area. She had been raped and murdered, picked to death at least twenty-four to forty-eight hours earlier; the body was frozen so they couldn't know for sure.

I mentioned it to him. "Jarnell, you won't believe this, but today I was watching the news and I saw an ice pick like the one you couldn't find this morning when you were trying to loosen the base of the gutter. They said it was found near the body of this lady. They think it might have been the murder weapon." He never looked up. I was excited and worried. "Jarnell what if that was ours? What if your prints are on it?" I said.

Jarnell got angry and started to yell.

"I didn't have anything to do with that! They sell those everywhere. I have an alibi. I was here with you when they found that body! I don't believe you don't believe me! I'm your husband!" he yelled.

I didn't understand. "What are you talking about? I didn't say anything like that. I know you wouldn't do anything like that. I'm thinking someone may have found it outside on the steps or something. Maybe we should call the police."

"We ain't calling no police. We ain't in it. We can't save all of the women in the world."

He was tired, I believed overworked and stressed.

Then the second woman was found almost two months later. She was bludgeoned to death with a blunt object. I said she should have fought. Jarnell said "She probably did, but how can you fight a bat, and the power of a man? A woman can't out power a man. I don't care how small or weak he seems."

"Oh, they said it was a bat? They didn't say that earlier."

"Well, they said blunt object. It had to be a bat or something like that."

"I guess you're right, if he caught her off guard there was probably nothing she could do. She was probably knocked out with the first blow."

"Or second," Jarnell said.

Turned out he was right, about the bat and the second blow. He was so smart, I thought. He should have been a detective instead of a telephone repairman.

Then there was the third and the fourth, both after only one month of no incident, both within three weeks of each other. The third was forty-five years old; older than the first and the second. The fourth was forty-four. It turned out they were connected—all of the women.

Each of the women were regular patrons of the ice cream shop on Eighty-seventh Street. At first I thought the owner was simply trying to get publicity for his store. *What a sick idea*, I thought when I saw him on the evening news. But when friends or family members of each woman verified what the store owner said about the ladies favoring his family special Chub Rock Triple Chunky Chocolate flavored ice cream, I was amazed. Yeah, Taylor's Cream was known for its original flavors, and yeah, people came from across and even out of town to purchase a scoop or more, but out of twenty-eight original flavors, all of the women who were killed frequently craved Chub Rock Triple Chunky Chocolate? Something was strange. Something was particularly weird when I found a pint of the stuff in our freezer. Jarnell never wanted Taylor's. It was almost as if he hated the place. I wasn't too fond of Chub Rock Triple Chunky Chocolate, it was too rich and gave me stomach aches, but I loved Peaches' Dream. It tasted almost like the Dreamsicle I loved as a kid; only it had chunks of peaches throughout.

"Jarnell, you eating Chub Rock Triple Chunky Chocolate now?" I asked when he arrived home, entered the kitchen and kissed me on my cheek. I didn't hug him as I normally would. My hands were wet and sticky. I was preparing his favorite, smothered chicken; it was his mother's recipe.

"No."

"No? There's a pint of it in the freezer. Who put it there?"

"I did."

"But you're not eating it? Did you buy it for me? You forgot my stomach can't handle all that chocolate?"

"No."

"Jarnell, you're acting rather strange now. You know that's the stuff all those women ate. You don't know if there's an ingredient that drives folks mad, in that stuff. Why of all times would you start eating it now?"

"I said I'm not eating it."

Then he left. That was the only time we spoke about it, but it remained, untouched; it's probably still there.

Then the psychic, the one I called instead of emailed because I didn't have a credit card, or an email address to receive the response, and I couldn't sign up for a free one to use at home, because Jarnell didn't like the internet, and I didn't know when Jarnell would have his next mandatory work meeting where I could sneak to the library and be sure he couldn't pop in and check on me; that psychic said she saw visions of chickens with their heads chopped off. I asked what she interpreted that to mean—chickens with their heads chopped off. She said it could mean an end was near. "An end to what?" My voice trembled; I couldn't help it.

"They run, in circles, they run, from and to nothing, they run…" is all she said. She never answered my question directly.

"So, is there a man around? Or women? Middle aged women? Or weapons? Or police?"

"There is a knife, and blood from the chickens, and breasts, and legs, and necks—long necks."

What in the hell?!, I planned to ask her, but I heard Jarnell's keys at the door. I quickly and quietly hung up the phone.

"Tamika. Could you give me a hand?" He was up front in the foyer. He had bags and bags of groceries. He placed them on the floor in the front doorway and I took them to the counter in the kitchen. This went on until my breaths grew short. Or had they come short after the headless chickens kept running through the lady's mouth, and my mind?

I calmed myself as I put the dairy and refrigerated products up first. Then I put the canned goods in the far left cabinet and the boxed items in the next cabinet over. Once all of the groceries were cleared, I grabbed a knife and the cutting board and began to chop the vegetables in preparation to bag and freeze them. Then in walked Jarnell with two more bags.

"I don't know how we left these, Tee. I've gotta run back to work." He grabbed an apple and bit into it. Mouth full of juice, apple, and red skin, he said "It's meat, baby, better get it in the freezer right away."

Five minutes later I was on the phone. I was crying, "chickens with heads chopped off... Jarnell why'd you buy chickens with heads chopped off?"

"It was all they had. Wings, thighs, and breasts were on sale, and sold out. I'm sorry, baby. I didn't know it mattered that much. All you have to do is cut them up. It's all really the same: breasts, legs—"

"And necks!" I cried.

"What is wrong with you, Tamika? Just throw the necks away That's what I do."

Jarnell threw necks away? Though we'd been together five years, there was so much I didn't know about him. *He threw necks away.* He'd said it himself.

Then there was the fifth woman. She was found just yesterday. Her neck was marked by some type of rope and she was strangled until she was nearly decapitated. It must have been cable cord. The cable cord Jarnell used at work was plastic and thin, yet, thick enough because it was laced with wires. So it could cut—like a wire would cut.

So I called from a pay phone—this afternoon. I wanted to ask the officer if they'd found cable cord near the forty-seven year old woman's body.

"No, no cable cord. Why ma'am? Do you have information relating to this murder?"

I didn't answer. I could be wrong about it all. It could be coincidence. So, I said nothing.

"Miss, do you have reason to believe you can identify someone who was involved with the murder?"

"You didn't find any cord? I thought the news said she was

strangled with some type of cord?"

"The markings on her neck are consistent with marks that would be made by some type of rope, or cord, but no cord was found at the site."

"No?"

"No. Forensics found fragments of some sort of thin string, but it has not yet been determined where it might have come from, or if it is even connected to the murder."

Jarnell surprised me. That evening he came in the house holding something behind his back. It was a Hello Kitty kite. "All we need is a stocking or something to make a tail. I've got string."

He placed an open, slightly used roll of thin string on the counter.

I passed out. I was dehydrated I told him when I came to; I hadn't been drinking enough water, I said. So he gave me water: loads of it, and I was bursting, full of lies, secrets, and water. And his hand across my belly made me uncomfortable because in the headphones I wore to shield him from the noise and the news, the reporter said there were new developments in the case. All of the murdered women were friends of a deceased woman who supposedly invented the secret recipe for Chub Rock Triple Chunky Chocolate ice cream. The woman who invented the ice cream sold the recipe to Mr. Taylor of Taylor's Cream more than twenty years ago. Then after spending the $500.00 recipe earnings on drugs, she committed suicide—hanging herself with thin rope. She was found by her single surviving son. The woman's name was Pamela Bleu and her son, his name was Jarnell Robertson.

It was Jarnell's mom.

Poor Jarnell, All these years he'd thought his mother had died of a heart attack. He told me he found her lying on the floor in their basement. I guess she fell after she hung herself. At nine years old there was no way he could've figured that out. The new news would surely crush him. I thought of waking him. I knew I should be the one to break the news. He would surely hear about it from someone, or on the radio while at work the next day. But he has been so tense and on edge lately I decided to let him sleep.

So I'm lying in this bed, Jarnell and me. I'm wondering why he never told me his mother invented the ice cream. I'm thinking it's both a shame she died so young, at twenty-seven, and a shame I'm glad she isn't alive to possibly be murdered by the weird psychopath who is killing all of her friends. Then a fleeting thought crosses my mind. *What if the murderer comes to kill Jarnell?* Then I tell myself to *Stop It! The murderer can't kill Jarnell. The murderer is—*

Then Jarnell moves. At the same time there is another news flash sounding off in my headphones. "The police are looking for Jarnell Robertson. He's wanted for questioning."

That's all, I think to myself. *They just want to ask him a few things.*

Jarnell is awake. His jaw is moving, so I remove the headphones to hear what he's saying to me. He isn't looking at me. He's staring in the other direction. I wonder if he's talking in his sleep. His voice is solid as if he's been awake a while. "Did I ever tell you I created a recipe for ice cream? I just mixed a bunch of stuff up. Everyone loved it. My mother stole it and sold it for a little bit of nothing to that snake Taylor."

One of the headphones is still on my ear, so I can hear the reporter and I can hear Jarnell. The reporter says security cameras at one of the women's residence show Jarnell entering the building the day the woman disappeared.

Jarnell is saying something about his mother ruining his future, and how he could have been rich and set for life had she not been so money hungry.

The reporter is saying Jarnell was also identified by a neighbor of one of the other women. The neighbor picked Jarnell out of a book, and said he was in a telephone repair truck and was wearing tools the morning she saw him enter her now dead neighbor's house.

Jarnell said he was so angry he wanted his mother dead.

The reporter said paint chips matching those on the ice pick were found in the telephone repair truck assigned to Jarnell.

Jarnell is saying, "Everyone but you has betrayed me. They know it is my recipe and yet, they go and buy it from him, as if it rightfully belongs to him."

Jarnell's voice is wound as tight as his arm is around my waist. I feel like I might pee on myself. I think, *It's been years since I wet the bed,* but I won't ask to be set free from him. I'm afraid. I think of the string. I hear the reporter saying how Jarnell's mother's death was mysterious, and police thought it may have been murder set up to look like suicide.

My fullness makes me dizzy. My head is pounding. Jarnell's voice is pounding; his words beating the air in our space.

"I ain't no punk!" He says. "People think because you're small you can just be messed over!"

He's pressing his face deep into his pillow. His words are muffled.

I think I hear knocking. It sounds like the front door. For the first time I notice the scissors on the night stand next to Jarnell by the bed. I have to pee. The knocking gets louder, almost thunderous. Jarnell seems not to notice, so I pretend it isn't happening; like it's all a dream.

"Jarnell, Honey, I need to use the washroom." I shake so he'll feel the urgency.

He looks at me.

"All that water you gave me." I smile.

"Huh?" He doesn't appear to understand; like he isn't even there, inside of himself.

"The water." I grab his arm gently. "Be careful, I might pee on myself." He and I lift his arm away from me and I jump up and run to the washroom down the hall. I could have used the washroom in the bedroom, but I didn't.

From the washroom in the hall, I can hear the banging clearly. I can also see the lights, circling through my home like a closed disco after all the people have gone. I look the door to the washroom and then wash my hands. *I'll let Jarnell handle it,* I think to myself, as I hold the wall and lower myself to the floor. After a few minutes I hear the crash. I think, *that was probably the front door*. Then after a few moments I hear Jarnell calling my name.

"Tamika! Stay here. Lock up. Don't you leave the house for nothing! Call a carpenter to fix the door. The money is in my bottom drawer."

I remain seated because I figure Jarnell's business doesn't involve me, plus I'm in my night gown.

"I'll be back!" He yells through grunts and what seems like struggle.

My body trembles. I imagine it's getting cold with the door removed in the middle of a late Chicago winter. *I wish I could get to the thermostat without being seen improperly dressed like this,* I think to myself. But I can't, so I sit and I tremble violently until the door crashes against the tub and the men rush in, asking if I'm alright. *I am,* but I don't say so aloud because Jarnell might be listening and I don't want him to leave me thinking I'm flirting in our house, in his favorite night gown, with strange men—I don't want him to think I'm unfaithful.

The Mark of Johnny-B-Gentle

With his life forcefully fitted into my rounded palm, his manhood mashed and swelling out between my knotted fingers, I could have killed him. I could have erased all the potential pain he would be sure to cause countless women. I could have in an instant made real his worst nightmare, making myself, a woman, his god. His very existence pulsed at my discretion.

He was a frightening sight to see. His spine and neck were more erect than his throbbing fully extended inflatable ego. His entire body seemed to fill and boil as if trying to explode. Tears spilled from his bubbling eyes. Beads of sweat connected on his brow and forehead, and ran like a narrow stream down the small of his back through the crack of his not-so-clean behind.

If he could have freed himself he would have killed me, or keeled himself over dead from the exhilaration of his fear. "Ba-by," he could barely manage through his trembling lips. I loosened my grip allowing blood to return to his brain. I wanted to hear what he would say. "Wha, wha, what's this a-bou—?" His head convulsed as his restrained body tried to eject the lump of vomit that clogged his throat. Partly digested dinner covered his broad shoulder and chiseled chest. It was green, speckled with flecks of orange and yellow. Healthy. Salad probably. His limp hands moved slightly surely wishing the grip of the handcuffs would somehow loosen, instead of tighten with motion. He looked wimpish.

A few days earlier I'd imagined he might have been 'the one.' He was handsome. He was articulate and smart, ambitious and successful. I'd met him about a month earlier in church. He was shy at first, almost afraid to speak. But he relaxed with familiarity. I made him feel at ease, he said, and then he grew to be quite aggressive. He had an unusual appetite for sex, which he explained was a result of infrequent sexual intimacy. He needed me to help him with his issues. He had a body full of fantasies—all which involved me and only me.

He loved me so much he wanted to experience everything with me. He wanted to use all of his resources, mind, body, soul, and finances to make us happy. He was an ideal creation, straight from the make-a-man factory—my special order.

Eventually, I found out he was no different than Mark, or Patrick, or Benny; all variances of the same, only Johnny's was concentrated. His was a potent dose of murderous lies, sex and intimacy.

During testimonials at church a couple of weeks ago, a tall, slim woman with the spirit of a wounded duck told of how God brought her to the church after first drawing her husband about a month ago. She had initially suspected he might have been cheating on her and she'd followed him, only to find out he was a good church going man: a man trying to correct the errors of his ways by sneaking away to the house of the Lord. Her husband was a changed man who made her believe in miracles and she stood up wanting to thank and praise God for Johnny, the same Johnny-B-Gentle I was expecting to marry.

Now I sat staring at him, gripping his pride firmer, coloring his face various shades of red, purple, then blue. Again, I could have killed him.

Thinking of the other woman, in the same before service testimonial, who spoke of another man from whom she'd contracted HIV, but still wanted to thank God she'd got a diagnosis early enough to have a chance at managing the effects on her body, I should have killed him. Hers was Johnny; John, she forgivingly called him.

Before the night would end, there would be at least four Johnnies who gave women cause to speak to the Lord. Four pieces of one in the same, one bastardly dude I was determined to help piece together. I knew by the language they used to describe him, the way they spoke of him; gently, as if he were fragile. I remembered his outward display of fragility, his pleading with me to have him unprotected sex. He needed me. He rambled about the red picket fence and home where he said we would someday raise our children. He needed to save a bit more money before he could acquire it. He wanted two dogs, and hoped that would be okay with me; two so one wouldn't be lonely. He was a soft dude whose only wish was to make everyone happy.

On the day that he rented us the room the desk clerk had called "regular" under his breath, Johnny-B-Gentle had no idea of how much happiness he would render. With my result paper in my purse, and the possibility of what it could have read on my mind, I followed him into the dingy motel room. That was almost two weeks ago.

I heard that when he was found four days after I left him, he was as small as his victims would be in their latter years, just before they would succumb to AIDS he'd knowingly shared. Rumors say the paramedics were perplexed as to the source of his bloodied wounds until they had carefully removed the stained and crusted mess to reveal the letters that had been etched into his belly—AIDS! Johnny, though alive, was, and has remained without speech. He couldn't, or wouldn't offer help as to the source of his victimization. Investigators estimated the weapon to have been a box cutter or scalpel. Nothing else could have managed such clean, deep, yet precise lines.

I almost killed him.

Had it not been for my religion I might have lost, I would have muzzled his breaths forever. But I didn't. Now his sighs and his pants haunt and chase me. I live marked as boldly and deeply as Johnny's belly. Someday he will probably find me. Someday he will do to me what I should have done to him. I know this, and I live like I'm sure of it.

Whining

Never paid attention to what his lying lips said, just heard his hands tell my waist he wished he'd met me sooner, and known me better. Heard the music thumping beneath his caged cry as we walked hand in hand to the dance floor.

Didn't know what my body had said to him when he was across the room, in the corner watching me as I stood near the bar. I know my eyes hadn't said a single thing to him directly, until he was near the back of my blouse, covering me ever so slightly, warming my skin in the already heated party.

Brass instruments, all artificially manufactured...

I think he asked my given name. Can't be sure of what the air said over and around my already rhythmically engaged tongue. Guess he knew my soul was called Symphony cause he seemed to play right into the rhythm.

Bass...

Could tell his soul was shy, had probably hid somewhere deep in the middle of his tall, solid frame for the bulk of its time it kept peeking and pushing out in bending elbows and bobbing hands. I wondered where it had been... before it was planted in such a fine edifice. I liked him, thought he was kinda cute, his soul.

Woodwind in the middle of a Lil' Wayne joint had to be for me and him…sounded real.

I was too old to know the lyrics of what I recognized as my son's favorite song, but I didn't need them. This guy, the conductor had confident hips that told me he didn't know the words either, but he was willing to work...

With the Percussions...

His back told my breast he was a hard working dude with lots of responsibility. He was straight most of the time, only bent forward or back a bit when the weight of the work weighed too heavy on him. Barely leaned on anyone, even me, just brushed cautiously needing to know someone was still there.

The hour at the sides of my middle stretched long winding beneath and beside his full frame, circling this dude like a velvet ribbon... winding, whining...

I hear you, guy. I know what they try to do to you. My knees on the edge of him, singing spontaneity, unregulated, unrehearsed. I watched them whisper to him. The crowd backed off giving us space, privacy. Heard my thighs get louder, saw them swell, braggingly tossing and catching my wide hips.

Saw my pelvis step to this dude, a would-be stranger, teasing and taunting him, telling him she's seen his gift, tucked compactly in the box where they told him to stay. She kept smiling and blushing, telling him his lid was loose and she was getting glimpses of him in the raw.

Strings...

She was pulling his strings, convincingly assuring him it was safe to come out and play.

The dee-jay spinned out of control. His soul spinned, the records played, soul music.

The beat slowed and I thought the guy would catch his breath and his mind, and compose himself and tidy his box and pack his stuff, relieved at having shaken loose some of the dust of the week, but... There were keys, and tinkling piano notes, and Donny Hathaway telling this warm man's arms and my hidden-in-his shoulders and neck we are alone, and I'm singing this song to you....

My ankles were reluctant to believe. They tried to leave the floor, but my toes, the spiked arches of my feet, and my made-taut calves held them there, anchored in this God-given thing, this unadulterated need, this staff where the notes of life were meant to be written.

His soul stood up, laid part of itself on breaths that warmed my scalp and mind, lined itself in flesh on leg bones and brushed through pants fabric and pantyhose, bent itself in fingers that gripped my hands while wrists barely and briefly brushed over the round of the bend in my butt... and my Symphony played like Miles would have liked it: jazzily wound and organic, not knowing what was coming, or what had already left, just in the moment, on top of and between the notes, whining about the week and the months and years without synchronized sound.

Then the lights came on. I had to climb out of him and his bandstand. The party was over. My friends and his friends were waiting, and somewhere between the dance floor and the valet line we gathered our coats and things, and remembered obligations: his paying my bar tab, me planning to pick up my daughter, his conversing—sealing a potential deal with a potential with a client, my being reminded to bring my best friend's romance novel to the next day six o'clock church service, and the box full of bugs I'd bought for the biology students in my class to watch, study and ultimately dissect, beginning Monday. All gurgles, drowning tunes.

Then, after my friends were situated in the car, right after new music had begun to burst through the speakers, seemingly rushing to get somewhere, or do something fast, just before I tucked myself into the back seat, the hairs on his face: eye brows, mustache and tiny goatee said he'd see me again. I don't know what broken ego-filtered words paraded from the open space between my lips, but I know my restless, trapped Symphony tapped a Morse-Code-like message on my spine, erecting my back and bosom. Can't be sure of what she said. Never mastered the codes, just occasionally heard the tapping.

Violins, harps, and acoustic guitars...

I wondered if he had been in the armed forces. Wondered if he understood the code and could have possibly translated it for me. Wondered if he could hear his own voice as loudly and clearly as I heard him. I never paid attention to what his lying lips said, just saw his slightly titled head complain about needing his tomorrows, heard his hands tell my waist he wished he'd met me sooner, and felt his ribs promise he wouldn't soon forget the way he conducted my Symphony.

Pretty Feet

Sometimes he asks her to come along. He never *has a seat*, never *waits for the next available attendant*. He prefers men; women are too slow. The water in the basin at the bottom of the vibrating pedicure chair is always too hot, too cold, too high, too bubbly. He wants the Asian attendant to sit off to the left of his reading angle. It's almost always a book about a woman's dysfunction, or a man's disdain for women with dysfunctions. He never reads real. He needs an apple juice or something from the vending machine. The cost is too much—should be included in the discount price of the clipping of nails and skin that has not yet fully grown back. The attendant should do him a favor and get the change, always exact, from his back jean pocket, and wash and dry his bubbly hands first, of course. The attendant never smiles. They always take too long—with him, and breathing, and fingertips occupying the time—hell, he only has two feet.

Finally, when he and she are at his house in the dark, after dinner and the movie he provides, after he's cleaned and put things in their proper places: the movie in its black Blockbuster case, the vertical paper towel holder in the right corner, flush with the crease of the right and left counters, her in his bed, on top of the top sheet, beneath the blanket under the spread, his lips evenly around the areola of her right breast, he finds what could be residual evidence of a hangnail on his left foot, the toe next to his pinky. It isn't painful, but still. He won't go back; he'll have to find another shop, another *five dollars off & free wax* on Tuesdays spot.

Sometimes she stays. This final time she's honest with herself—his feet are too pretty.

Printed in the United States
125359LV00003B/1-357/P

9 780883 783023